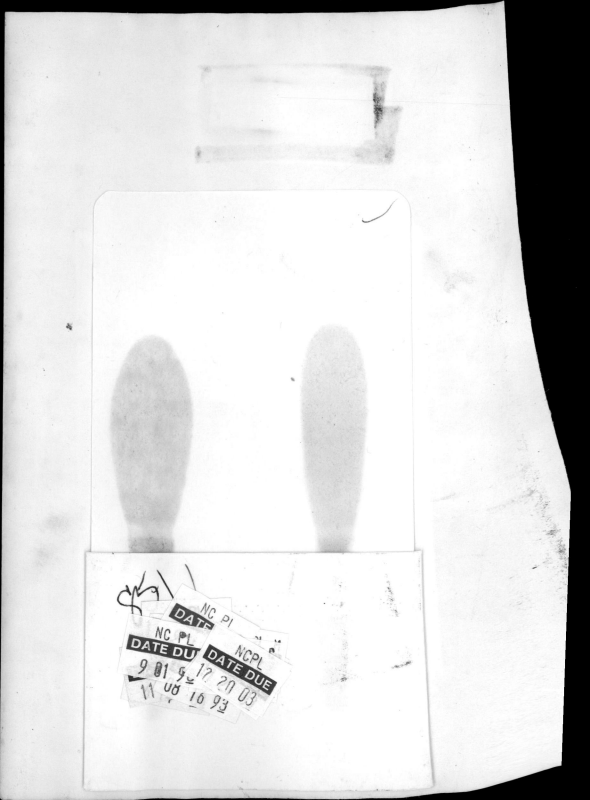

THE MARQUIS WHO HATED WOMEN

BARBARA CARTLAND

The Marquis Who Hated Women

DURON BOOKS

1977

153 p

THE MARQUIS WHO HATED WOMEN
A Duron Book / May 1977

ISBN 0-87272-065-9

Duron Books are published by Brodart Inc. Its trademark, consisting
of the words "Duron Books" and the portrayal of a Duron, is regis-
tered in the United States Patent Office and in other countries.

PRINTED IN THE UNITED STATES OF AMERICA

THE MARQUIS WHO HATED WOMEN

Chapter One

1853

"It is getting late. I must go."

The Marquis turned over as he spoke and started to rise from the bed.

Inez Shangarry gave a little cry of protest.

"Oh, no, Osborne, no! You cannot leave me so soon. I want you!"

The Marquis shook himself free of her clinging arms and started to put on his discarded clothes.

Lying back against the pillows with her dark hair falling over her naked body, Lady Shangarry made an enticing picture.

"You cannot leave me, you cannot!" she said. "It is still very early and there are so few evenings when we can be together like this."

There was a glint of fire in her eyes and her red lips pouted provocatively.

"You are very persuasive, Inez," the Marquis said as he moved across the room to the dressing-table to pick up his discarded cravat.

"I want to be persuasive, and I want to be with you—you know that," Lady Shangarry said in a low, seductive voice, "but it is difficult sometimes. When we are alone together I know that you are the most attractive and the most perfect lover any woman could desire."

1

The Marquis tied his black cravat with experienced fingers. Then as he reached for his evening-coat he turned to look back at the silk-draped bed and its attractive occupant.

"I am going to the country tomorrow," he said, "and as I wish to leave early I think it important for me to have my 'beauty sleep,' just as you will need yours."

"That is far from a compliment," Inez Shangarry said petulantly. "I want you to stay with me. Surely, Osborne, after all we have meant to each other, you can grant me just a few more minutes of your time?"

"I hardly think it would be just a few minutes," the Marquis said in an amused voice.

It was in fact difficult to believe that any man could resist the allurements of Lady Shangarry, who was recognised as having the most perfect figure in the whole of London.

She was acclaimed by all the connoisseurs of beauty, including Rakes, Rués, and men like the Marquis who were noted as being extremely particular in their choice of female companionship.

The Marquis was well aware not only of his reputation for being fastidious, but also that almost every woman at whom he looked with any favour was only too willing to fall into his arms.

He had however resisted the allurements of Lady Shangarry for some time, although he knew that she was manoeuvring for him with the confidence of a woman who has found that few men can resist her.

Finally, because she was not only beautiful but also because she amused him, he had succumbed to the invitation she expressed in every look in her eyes, in every movement of her voluptuously curvey body.

Now, because she was so insistent on his staying longer than he wished, he wondered if in fact she was not becoming somewhat of a bore and if the end of their liaison was already in sight.

The Marquis was noted for being completely ruthless where his love-affairs were concerned.

He preferred to do his own hunting, but unfortunately the chase was always brief, since the objects of his attention made little effort to escape him.

All too quickly any woman in whom he was interested settled into a familiar pattern of becoming clinging and demanding.

At thirty-three the Marquis had resisted every possible trick and trap to entice him up the aisle into respectable matrimony, and preferred women already married, who relieved the boredom of their lives with a continuous succession of lovers.

The result was of course that he was disliked violently and aggressively by a large number of husbands, and as one wag put it: "The Marquis has only to appear in any Assembly to raise the blood-pressure to apoplectic intensity of half the men present!"

Although various threats had been made against him, no-one so far had managed to catch the Marquis red-handed.

He was so discreet and so careful in public that rumours concerning his love-affairs rested only on conjecture and surmise rather than on any actual proof to betray him.

"Darling—you are the most handsome man I have ever seen!" Inez Shangarry said from the bed.

"I am flattered, Inez," the Marquis said, but his tone was cynical.

"I mean it," she said insistently, "and that is why I want to kiss you. Come here! You cannot refuse me one last kiss."

She held out her white arms as she spoke, but the Marquis laughed and shook his head.

"I have been caught that way before!"

He was only too well aware that if a man bent over a woman in bed and she pulled him down upon her, he was helpless. He was sure that that was Inez Shangarry's intention and it made him all the more determined to escape.

She was insatiable, he thought. She did not seem tired after the fierceness of their love-making, while

he himself felt a definite reaction that made him wish
to be free of the warm, scented room.

There was the heavy fragrance of flowers min-
gled with an exotic perfume which Inez Shangarry always used, and which her lovers found lingered on
their clothes long after they had left her presence.

There was no doubt, the Marquis thought, that
she was exceptionally beautiful. At the same time,
there was something lacking to which he could not
put a name.

She could make him laugh by the sharpness of her
wit, which most other women failed to do; but although their association was fiery and tempestuous he
knew that he was not in the least in love with her.

In fact, as usual his heart was completely un-
touched, so that if he never saw her again it would
have not troubled him in the slightest.

"I must go, Inez," he said. "Thank you for an enchanting evening, and I hope we shall be able to dine
together very soon in the near future."

He took her hand as he spoke and lifted it to his
lips, but as he did so her fingers tightened on his and
she said insistently:

"Kiss me, Osborne, stay with me a little longer! I
want you—I need you! I cannot let you leave me!"

There was such a passionate note in her voice, together with an almost frantic determination to keep
him, that the Marquis looked at her in surprise.

As he did so he heard a faint sound from the
room below them. It was very faint, but he knew that
Inez Shangarry had heard it too. Then she held on to
him even more tightly and her voice rose a little as she
said:

"I love you, Osborne! I love you! Kiss me! Please
kiss me."

The Marquis freed himself from her, and moving
swiftly across the room went not to the door which led
to the landing but through another, which opened
into a dressing-room occupied by Lord Shangarry
when he was at home.

The room was in darkness but the Marquis crossed it in a few steps and pulled back the curtains over the window.

It was a starlit night with the moon appearing fitfully between drifting clouds.

The Marquis flung up the window to look out.

As he expected, there was a drop of about twelve feet onto a roof below and again a long drop from there to the Mews.

Without wasting any time he let himself down by his arms, and then with his body fully outstretched he dropped lightly and with athletic expertise onto the roof beneath him.

Once there he climbed over the edge, and this time with the help of a drainpipe descended onto the rough cobbles of the Mews.

He heard the sleeves of his evening-coat splitting at the armholes as he did so, but then his tailor had never envisaged his indulging in such acrobatic feats when he was dressed for dinner.

The shadows in the deserted Mews were dark and the Marquis moved quickly from where he was standing into the darkness created by one of the stable doors. Then he looked up at the window he had left behind him.

He did not have to wait more than a few seconds.

At the open aperture the head of a man, who leant out and looked searchingly at the roof beneath the window, then into the Mews.

The Marquis kept very still. He recognised Lord Shangarry quite clearly and he knew that he had just escaped from a cleverly and well-baited trap.

It must have been some sixth sense, he thought, that had made him feel that Inez's insistence on his staying longer had been over-acted, and perhaps he had a special perception where women were concerned.

He had thought for some time that Inez's desire to possess him was growing to the point where it could be dangerous.

He well knew that if, as she had intended, her husband had found them making love, there were only two courses open.

The first was that Shangarry should divorce her, in which case she would eventually become the Marchioness of Linwood, and however great the penalties of scandal and social ostracism the ultimate result would justify them.

Alternatively, and the Marquis could not help thinking this might be more likely, Lord Shangarry would demand a very large sum of money to assuage his outraged feelings and soothe his pride.

Watching him staring from the open window, the Marquis was quite certain that the plot had been concocted between them.

Now, when he thought of it, he remembered someone at the Club saying that Shangarry was deeply in debt, and from things that Inez had told him he was certain that they were finding it hard to make ends meet.

What then could be better from their standpoint than to be in a position to blackmail—discreetly, of course—someone as rich as himself?

They knew he would not wish to be involved in anything so unsavoury as a Court Case, and he could certainly afford to pay handsomely for his misdemeanours.

"I have been a fool!" the Marquis told himself.

Then, as Lord Shangarry, cheated of his prey, slammed the window shut, he cursed beneath his breath.

"Damn the woman! Damn all women! I hate them all—I always have!"

The violence he felt surprised even himself, and yet it was in part true. He did dislike women as a sex.

Although he used them for his own ends, finding a fleeting and very transitory pleasure in their company when they surrendered themselves to his desires, he had never met a woman whose companionship he preferred to that of a man or whom he left with any sense of regret.

The way Inez had behaved tonight, he thought, was typical of the female of the species.

Looking back, he could see how she had gradually inveigled her way into his consciousness, and how the mere fact that all other men sang her praises had made him feel that she was more desirable than in fact she was.

When it came down to it, she was very like every other woman to whom he had made love, and there was nothing at all unique about her.

Now he could only curse himself for being as brainless as any unfledged youth in letting himself nearly be caught in a situation from which it would have been impossible to extricate himself with any dignity.

"Curse them—curse them both!" the Marquis swore.

Then after waiting until he was quite certain Lord Shangarry was no longer peering through the window, he turned and started to walk up the Mews.

In the stables as he passed them he could hear the sound of horses moving restlessly in their stalls, and occasionally the whistling of a groom who had been kept out late and was rubbing down his animals before he himself went to bed.

There were the smells of leather, hay, and hores-flesh, which the Marquis knew well.

It made him think of the country and conjured up in him a sudden longing to be free of London and the social gossip and intrigue, which he disliked, especially if it concerned himself

He had walked quite a little way before he stopped suddenly as it came to his mind that however skilfully he had escaped from the Shangarry house he had left two pieces of incriminating evidence behind— his hat and his evening-cloak.

He had not thought of them until the January

wind blowing down the Mews made him shiver and he felt the frost in the air against his bare forehead.

Shangarry would have seen both objects in the Hall, and undoubtedly he would be discussing with his wife at the moment how they could be turned to their advantage.

The Marquis gritted his teeth angrily.

Why, he asked himself, had he not been more suspicious when Inez Shangarry had told him so glibly that her husband would be away from London that evening?

"Patrick is going to visit some friends at Epsom," she had said. "He wants to look at their horses and it will be too late for him to return tonight since it is dark so early."

It had seemed quite a plausible story at the time. But now the Marquis told himself he must have been extremely stupid to think that any man who cared for his wife would leave her alone in London when he must have been aware who her escort would be in his absence.

"I underestimated my own reputation," he told himself, "which is something I do not do as a rule."

There was nothing he could do about it now, but as he walked on he thought with fury of his hat and evening-cloak with its red satin lining reposing on a mahogany chair in the narrow, unimpressive Hall.

He remembered how, when they came back from the Restaurant where they had dined in a private room so that they would not be seen together, their desire for each other leaping like a flame had made Inez hurry him upstairs without even stopping in the Drawing-Room for the usual glass of wine.

Now he thought he could distinctly remember her saying, "Leave your things there," and almost automatically he had put down his hat and swung his cloak from his shoulders.

Then she had led the way upstairs, her full skirts moving seductively against the bannisters, her neck and shoulders gleaming white in the dim, lowered gas-lights.

"I deserve everything that comes to me!" the Marquis said savagely to himself. "At my age, with my experience, I should have learnt to trust no-one—let alone a woman!"

His self-accusation did not make him feel any warmer and he moved more briskly, coming to the end of the Mews and turning into another street where the houses faced onto the pavement.

He had not gone more than a few yards when suddenly something fell at his feet with a thud and instinctively he jumped backwards, knowing that if it had hit him on the head it would have laid him out.

He looked down and saw that it was a valise, an elegant, expensive valise such as ladies carried when they travelled in a coach or a railway-carriage.

The Marquis stared at it in surprise. Then as he raised his head to look from where it had come he heard a voice crying: "Help! Help!"

He looked up and saw to his astonishment that just above his head a woman was swinging on a rope.

Her full skirts billowed out and they seemed to keep her suspended in mid-air.

Then he realised that her predicament lay in the fact that the rope was not long enough. It did not reach the ground and was short by at least six feet.

"Help!" she called again. "Help!"

Without thinking what he was doing, the Marquis stepped forward to reach up his arms, and clasping her above the ankles he held her steady.

He realised she was very light, and having a firm grip on her he said:

"You can let go now, I will not let you fall."

She must have obeyed him, for he felt her bend over to try to put her hands on his shoulders and he let her slide slowly down, holding her finally round the waist until her feet were on the ground.

As he did so he realised that she was dressed expensively in silk, and she had a faint fresh scent which reminded him of spring flowers.

Then as he released her she started to smooth her skirts into place and pull down the sleeves of the tight-fitting jacket she wore.

"Thank you," she said. "I was afraid the rope would not be long enough, but I had to take a chance."

"What has happened to the gentleman who should be assisting you to elope?" the Marquis asked with an amused note in his voice. "Surely he should be here by now?"

"It is nothing like that!" the woman replied sharply.

Now by the light of the moon he could see that she was very young, only a girl, and when the wind lifted the brim of her bonnet he could see a small, pointed face and what he thought were very large eyes.

"You are not eloping?" he enquired.

"No, of course not! I am running *away* from a man, not *to* one!" she said. "If you want to know the truth, I hate men! I hate all of them!"

The Marquis laughed and when she looked at him in surprise he explained:

"That is a sentiment I have just been expressing to myself, except that in my case I was hating women!"

She did not appear to be interested in his explanation but bent down to pick up her valise.

It was almost too heavy for her, but she took hold of it with both hands and there was something so immature about her figure that the Marquis said:

"If you are intent on running away alone, I should think again. You will not be able to manage without someone to look after you! So be a good girl, go home and think it over. I do not suppose things are as bad as you suspect."

"I have no intention of doing that."

"Then doubtless it is my duty to make you," the Marquis replied.

She gave a little cry and dropped the valise—this time on the edge of his foot. Then, before he could realise what was happening, she was running down the road away from him, moving with a swiftness which made her skirts fly out behind her.

"Hi! Stop!" the Marquis shouted. "It is nothing to do with me. Stop, I tell you!"

He picked up the valise preparatory to running after her, but at that moment he saw someone emerge from the shadows at the end of the street and he heard the girl give a cry of fear.

Moving quickly and carrying the valise, which was in fact quite heavy, the Marquis hurried to where the girl who had run away from him was struggling.

He saw that it was with one of the ragged men who hung about the streets at all times of the day and night in the hope of earning a few pence for holding a horse or, doubtless, if the opportunity arose, of picking a pocket.

"Oi've got 'er, Guv'nor. Oi'll 'old on to 'er!" the man said as the Marquis approached.

"Let me go! How dare you touch me?" the girl was saying furiously, pulling and trying to free her hand, which the man was holding with both of his.

"Let her go!" the Marquis said in a tone of authority.

He took a coin from his pocket and threw it on the ground.

"Now be off with you!"

The man bent down to snatch up the coin and did as he was told.

As the girl stood rubbing her wrists the Marquis said quietly:

"There is no need to run away from me. What you do is not my business, but I think you see already that there are certain pit-falls for young women who move about the streets alone at this time of the night."

"I had hoped to find a hackney-carriage."

"There might be one in Grosvenor Square," the

Marquis said. "That is where I am going, and if you wish I will carry your valise for you."

"Thank you," the girl said. "I thought there might have been a hansom on the rank in Berkeley Square."

She paused, then added:

"As a matter of fact, I have never been in a hansom. That will be an adventure in itself!"

"If you are looking for adventure," the Marquis said, "I can think of less dangerous ones than walking about London in the middle of the night."

"I am not doing it for pleasure!" she retorted sharply. "I have to escape! If I stay . . ."

She stopped speaking, as if she felt she was being too confiding, and they walked on in silence.

The wind that met them round the corner of Carlos Place made the Marquis shiver and he realised that his companion was shivering too.

"Surely you should have brought a cloak with you?" he asked.

"I have a shawl in my valise," she answered, "but it would not have been easy to come down the rope with anything over my shoulders."

"No, of course not," he said. "It is a somewhat uncomfortable way of leaving one's residence."

"The night-footman sits in the Hall," the girl said as if she thought he was being very dense, "and I thought if I tried to let myself out by the area door one of the servants would hear me. Another footman sleeps in the Pantry."

"I can understand your predicament!"

She heard the laughter in his voice and said angrily:

"It may seem amusing to you, but I have had to think this out very carefully, and when I thought you were going to upset all my plans I naturally had to run away."

"Naturally!" the Marquis agreed.

"Now all I want is a hackney-carriage."

"Where do you want to go?" the Marquis enquired. "The cabmen are usually unwilling to drive far at this time of the night."

"I am going to Egypt."

"To Egypt?"

The Marquis repeated the word in astonishment.

"I am going to find my father."

"And you really intend to travel there alone?"

"There is no-one to go with me," she said, "and I must catch a very early train to Southampton before my Uncle finds out that I have disappeared."

The Marquis turned to look at her in surprise. As he did so, his own predicament suddenly came to his mind and he envisaged a possible solution.

His yacht lay at Southampton, and if he left London before Shangarry could call on him to return his hat and cloak and ask the explanation for their presence in his house, it would mean that he was definitely "off the hook."

He followed up his train of thought and it seemed quite clear that once he was away from England the Shangarrys would have to find some other fool to pay their bills.

It would undoubtedly be impossible for them to await his return if their creditors were as pressing as he had been led to believe.

That, he thought with a sense of triumph, was exactly what he would do.

He would take his yacht at once to the Mediterranean, as he had intended to do anyway in a month or so.

No-one would be surprised. Shooting was over; there was too much frost for hunting; and the fact that he left London in January would not invite a query as to his reason for doing so.

What was more, the Marquis told himself, it would definitely be a score off Inez Shangarry and her crooked scheming!

"Damnit all, that is what I will do!" he said beneath his breath, and remembered that he was not alone.

"Did you say something?" his companion asked.
"Only to myself," he replied.

They had reached Grosvenor Square by this time
and when the Marquis looked at the place near the
garden where there was usually a line of hackney-
carriages drawn by tired, underfed horses, there was
not one to be seen.

"I suppose really it is too late at night," the girl
beside him said nervously.

"I am afraid it is," the Marquis agreed. "But I
have a suggestion to make which you might find help-
ful."

"What is that?" she asked.

"I intend leaving London myself this morning,"
he said. "It happens that I also shall be leaving from
Southampton, and I have to find out about the
trains."

He stopped as he spoke, having reached his
house, to continue:

"The direct line, as I expect you know, is from
Nine Elms, the station before Clapham Junction. If
you would like to wait while I look them up in Bradshaw, I dare say my footmen will be able to procure
a hackney-carriage which will take you to the station."

"Why can I not go with you?" the girl asked.

The Marquis looked at her as she spoke, and by
the light of the moon that had come out from behind
a cloud she saw the surprise on his face.

"I am . . . sorry," she said humbly. "I realise I
should not have suggested that."

"I think it quite a sensible suggestion," the Marquis replied, "and forgive me, I should have thought
of it myself, but I am not used to meeting young
women who wish to travel to Egypt!"

"I am quite used to travelling," the girl said almost antagonistically. "You need not worry about me."

"I am not," the Marquis answered, "but if it
would be of any help to you I shall of course be delighted to escort you to the station."

He walked to the door as he spoke.

It was a large, impressive house and his companion looked at it somewhat doubtfully before she said:

"I suppose I ought not . . . really to come . . . into
your house with you . . . alone."

"If you are worried about the propriety of it," the
Marquis answered, "I see in that little difference from
your leaving your own home on the end of a rope, and
if you are nervous as to my intentions, may I inform
you that I spoke the truth when I said I hate women!"

"Just as I hate men," she said, and he thought the
smile on her lips was rather attractive.

"Then we are of accord in that sentiment if in
nothing else," the Marquis said. "I think you would be
wise to come inside rather than stand in this cold,
which might easily lead to pneumonia."

"Thank you," his companion said with dignity.
"As a matter of fact, I do feel frozen."

The Marquis knocked on the door, which was
opened almost immediately by his footman who had
been sitting in a round-topped padded chair in the
Hall.

He looked surprised at seeing his master without
his hat or cape, apparently on foot and carrying a valise.

The Marquis put the valise into the footman's
hand.

"I want warm drinks, James, and something to eat
brought to the Library," he said. "Tell Hignet to attend me there."

"Very good, M'Lord."

The Marquis walked across the Hall and opened
a door at the end of it.

The girl preceded him into a large Library which
looked out onto the garden at the back of the house.

There were several lights burning and the footman who had followed them into the room turned up
the gas. It was a comfortably furnished room, lined
with books and showing every evidence of luxury and
wealth.

The Marquis walked across to his desk and

opened several drawers before he found what he
sought. Then he came to the fireplace, where the girl
was crouching down, holding out her hands to the
fire.

"It was very silly of me not to bring a cloak," she
said. "Now that I think about it, I could have thrown
it out of the window with my valise."

"As that missed me only by inches," the Marquis
replied, "to find myself suddenly enveloped in the
folds of a heavy cloak might have been quite unnerving!"

"I did not expect anyone to be about at that time
of night."

She looked up at him and he saw that he had not
been mistaken in thinking that she was pretty and
that her eyes were large.

They did in fact seem to fill her face, large, dark
grey eyes, and she seemed very slender and frail in
the firelight.

"Now suppose we introduce ourselves?" the Marquis said. "I confess to being curious as to why you
are setting out on this long and arduous journey by
yourself."

"My name is Shikara Bartlett."

"Shikara?" the Marquis repeated. "It is a name I
have never heard before."

"It is Indian," she explained. "My father was ex-
ploring parts of India just before I was born, and
Mama said he was determined that I should have an
Indian name because he found them so attractive."

"Your father is an Explorer?"

"No, he is an Archaeologist."

"Of course!" the Marquis exclaimed. "Professor
Richard Bartlett. I have heard of him. I read the book
he wrote on his finds in Persia."

"Papa is famous," Shikara said, "but I have not
heard from him for nearly nine months, and I am worried . . . very worried as to what could have happened to him."

"You say he is in Egypt?"

"Yes. He went off last spring to meet a man called Auguste Mariette, who had made some sensational discoveries near the Pyramids. He wrote to Papa about it, who of course decided to leave at once! So he asked his brother, Sir Hardwin Bartlett, with whom we were staying, to look after me."

"I think I have met Sir Hardwin," the Marquis said, knitting his brow.

"I am sorry for you if you have," Shikara said. "He is a horrible, pig-headed, obstinate man and I hate him! If I had any sense I would have murdered him before I left!"

"That sounds very blood-thirsty!" the Marquis laughed.

"It is all very well for you to laugh," Shikara said crossly, "but you do not know what I have suffered living with him."

She took off her bonnet as she was speaking and now the Marquis saw that she had fair hair in which there were golden lights.

The flames leaping in the fireplace seemed to pick them out and make them shine and he realised that in fact Shikara was not only pretty but had a strange, unusual loveliness that he had never encountered before

"Whatever your Uncle is like," he said, "surely it is rather drastic to run away as you are doing, having no idea of the difficulties in which you may find yourself without anyone to look after you?"

"No difficulties could be worse than trying to persuade Uncle Hardwin that I have no intention of marrying Lord Stroud!"

"Stroud?" the Marquis ejaculated. "He is a member of my Club, but he is old!"

"Forty-four to be exact!" Shikara said. "But Uncle Hardwin thinks he would be a stable, restraining influence on me, and as my Guardian he tells me that I have no choice in the matter . . . that I have to marry him."

"That I agree is ridiculous," the Marquis said.

"You are much too young to be married to a man of Stroud's age."

He remembered coming across Lord Stroud at various Parliamentary parties, and he had spoken to him in White's.

He had always thought of him as a heavy, boring man who was prepared to pontificate at length on any subject and to lay down the law without listening to anyone else's opinion.

"You see, the trouble is that I am an heiress," Shikara said confidingly.

The Marquis raised his eye-brows and she went on:

"I know it is vulgar to talk about money, but I do not suppose Lord Stroud, or the other men who have been pursuing me so ardently, would be so keen if Uncle Hardwin had not told them that I will be wealthy when I come of age."

"I think perhaps you are under-rating your personal attractions," the Marquis said with a twist of his lips.

"I suppose it makes it a better proposition if I am 'twopence coloured' rather than 'a penny plain,'" Shikara retorted. "I know they want to get their greedy hands on the hundred thousand pounds which my mother left me when she died."

"That is quite a fortune!" the Marquis agreed.

"That is what *they* think," Shikara said, "but I am not going to marry any of them, whatever Uncle Hardwin may do to me!"

"What do you mean by that?" the Marquis enquired.

"Oh, he has threatened to beat me, to shut me in my room with only bread and water. He has used every threat in the calendar, but I will not give in to him . . . I will not! Not if it kills me!"

She spoke so violently that the Marquis could not help smiling. She was so small and fragile and yet she was snarling like a tigress.

Then he realised that from his point of view he

would make a great mistake if he became involved in Shikara's predicament.

It was one thing to defend a young girl who had descended on him literally from the sky above, but quite another to be involved in helping an heiress to escape from her lawful Guardian.

"Surely you must have other relatives you could go to?" he asked tentatively.

"If they would have me . . . which I doubt," Shikara replied. "They are all much too frightened of Uncle Hardwin to go against his wishes. He is the head of the family. Papa has always said that you might as well beat your head against the Rock of Gibraltar as try to make him change his mind about anything."

She paused, then said in a low voice:

"He is determined that I shall marry Lord Stroud, but I loathe him! I would sooner be touched by a reptile!"

"I can understand that," the Marquis agreed. "At the same time . . ."

He stopped.

He decided he would not argue with Shikara, but he would make it quite clear that her problem had nothing to do with him, that he would not be involved.

He opened the Bradshaw Guide, which he held in his hand, turned the pages, and after a moment said:

"I see there is a fast train leaving Nine Elms at seven A.M. It reaches Southampton at nine-fifty. That means we should have to leave here at about six o'clock."

"Is there no earlier one?" Shikara asked. "The house-maids get up at five-thirty and someone may see the rope dangling from my window."

"There is one at six-thirty," the Marquis said, his eyes on the guide-book, "but it does not get to Southampton any earlier, as it stops at every station on the way."

"Then I suppose I had better chance it," she said. "He would hardly look for me here."

"I think it is unlikely," the Marquis agreed. "If you travel in my carriage I think it equally unlikely that your Uncle will suspect that I am your escort."

"You are right," she said. "Thank you. That is what I would like to do."

The door opened and the Marquis's valet came into the room.

"You wanted me, M'Lord?"

He spoke in a quiet, unhurried tone, as if it was quite usual for him to be awakened in the middle of the night and brought downstairs.

"Yes, Hignet," the Marquis answered. "We are leaving for Southampton at six o'clock. We shall join the yacht. Pack everything I will require.

"Hot or cold weather, M'Lord?"

"I might go to the Mediterranean, or perhaps Morocco," the Marquis answered.

"Very good, M'Lord."

"As it seems unnecessary to awaken Mrs. Kingdom," the Marquis said, "perhaps you would show this young lady to one of the bed-rooms where she can wash and tidy herself. I have asked for some hot drinks and food. I presume it is being prepared?"

"The Chef has been notified, M'Lord," Hignet answered. "And you'll require food for the journey. Shall I prepare a hamper for two?"

The Marquis hesitated a moment, then said:

"Two hampers, Hignet. The young lady would prefer, I am sure, to travel in a carriage reserved for ladies only."

"Very good, M'Lord."

Hignet waited and Shikara carrying her bonnet moved to stand beside him.

"Ask Hignet for anything you want," the Marquis said.

"Thank you," she replied.

When he was alone, the Marquis stood looking

down into the fire and his thoughts returned immediately to his own problem.

He was quite certain that the only sensible thing to do was, as he had decided, to leave the country. At the same time, it annoyed him that he should have to sacrifice his pride and run away.

Yet the alternative was even more humiliating, since he was quite certain that Shangarry would extort every possible penny from him while at the same time being quite prepared to blackguard him to his friends.

This, he told himself, would teach him to be more careful with whom he associated in the future. If he needed a woman he would be far better to keep to Cyprians.

He had always disliked associating with Cocottes; for the fact that their favours were dispensed entirely for money had always seemed to him to be definitely unpleasant.

Now he asked himself if there was really any difference between women who frankly charged for their services and society women who expected jewels, or any other object that took their fancy, in return for their so-called love.

The whole thing, the Marquis thought, disgusted him, and almost like Shikara he found himself delighted at the idea of leaving London, of being free of the social octopus which seemed to be clutching at him with a thousand different tentacles.

He thought with pleasure of his new yacht which was waiting for him at Southampton. It was indeed a blessing that it had been delivered a month ago.

He had been looking forward to trying it out, and although he had not envisaged anything so unpredictable as the seas in January, there was every likelihood that the Bay of Biscay might be no worse than in March or in April.

"No-one can be sure of the weather at any time of the year," the Marquis told himself.

He remembered with satisfaction that however rough the seas might be, neither he nor Hignet would be sick.

They had travelled together to many different parts of the world and the Marquis knew that however many snags they might encounter during the journey, Hignet would always remain the same, unflappable, resourceful, and always prepared to make the best of any situation.

Quite suddenly he found himself feeling like a school-boy leaving for the holidays.

"I will go to one of the Arab countries," he decided. "There it is a man's world, where they have the sense to keep their women shut up in purdah and covered up to the eyes so that they are no temptation to anyone else."

He laughed, knowing at the same time that it would take him a long time to get over the situation in which he had just found himself, very nearly out-manoeuvred by a woman.

He was still thinking of Inez Shangarry when the door opened and Shikara returned.

She had taken off her jacket and now she wore a shawl round her shoulders.

It covered a muslin blouse inset with lace and made her look very young and even more slender and fragile than before.

Instinctively the words came to the Marquis's lips to remonstrate with her that she should let him take her back to her Guardian and not embark on such a crazy escapade.

Then he told himself to keep his mouth shut and not concern himself with someone who could not by any flight of imagination have any claim on his attention. He had met Shikara by sheer chance and that was all there was to it!

She had been followed into the room by two footmen carrying a table, which they set down near the fire.

"The Chef asks your indulgence, M'Lord," one of them said to the Marquis. "But, thinking Your Lordship might be in a hurry, he has prepared simple dishes which took him the minimum amount of time. He hopes Your Lordship will not be disappointed."

"I dare say we shall manage," the Marquis conceded.

The second footman opened a bottle of wine and the Marquis tasted it and nodded his head.

"I hope you will drink a little claret, Miss Bartlett," he said to Shikara. "It will take away the cold and give you strength for your journey."

"As a matter of fact, I am very hungry," Shikara replied. "I had a row with Uncle Hardwin before dinner and refused to dine with him, and naturally he would not pander to me by sending anything up to my room."

"Make up for it now," the Marquis suggested, noting with satisfaction that despite the Chef's apologies there seemed to be quite a number of silver dishes being placed on a side-table.

There was in fact so much to eat that long before the last course had been presented Shikara protested she could eat no more.

"Hignet will see that you have a hamper in your carriage to Southampton," the Marquis said, "and as we arrive so early you will doubtless find a ship sailing sometime during the day. I am afraid Bradshaw does not give us a sailing list."

"I will find one," Shikara said confidently, "and once I am at sea, I shall really feel free of Uncle Hardwin."

"Are you frightened of him?" the Marquis asked. "You do not seem to be the sort of person who would be frightened of anything or anybody."

"As a matter of fact, he does frighten me," Shikara said in a small voice. "He is so very big, and when he says that he will beat me if I do not marry Lord Stroud I know he means it"

"Surely your father would not approve of that?"

"No, of course not! Papa is the kindest person that one could ever imagine."

She smiled and it was rather wistful.

"Unfortunately, he keeps forgetting my existence when he gets excited about some woman he has dug up in a tomb, who lived three thousand years ago, or a carved animal that has lost a leg and its head as well!"

The Marquis smiled.

"That must be somewhat frustrating, but unfortunately it is the penalty a daughter must pay when she has a famous father."

"I only wish I knew what has happened to him," Shikara said. "I wrote to *Monsieur* Mariette, but I feel he could not have received my letter, and Uncle Hardwin says he is quite certain that Papa is dead!"

"Why should he be sure of that?"

"Because Papa always wrote to me at least once a month ... he never missed ... just the same as he wrote to Mama every week when he left her to go exploring."

"I understand your mother is dead."

"Yes, she died three years ago. I know that if she were alive she would not let Uncle Hardwin bully me into marrying anyone I did not ... love."

"But I thought you hated men?" the Marquis questioned. "Yet you are hoping to love someone."

"I shall never love a man," Shikara said positively. "I hate them when they try to bully me, and I hate them when they have that stupid, swimmy look in their eyes and want to touch me."

She gave a little sigh.

"When I told Uncle Hardwin that, he said I was unnatural; but I cannot see why one should say one likes people if one does not, and men repel me ... every one of them.

"I suppose really I should feel affronted when you say that," the Marquis said.

She looked at him and he thought to his surprise

that she was considering him as a man for the first time.

"But you are different because you say you hate women," she replied. "If you tried to bully me or look at me in a sloppy sort of way I would hate you too!"

"I will be very careful to do neither!"

"Now you are laughing at me again," Shikara said accusingly. "But as we shall never see each other after we reach Southampton, I see no reason why I should not tell you the truth."

"I prefer the truth in such circumstances."

Putting her arm on the table and resting her hand on her chin, she looked at him reflectively and said:

"I wonder if you really mean that. I have a feeling that you are used to women making a fuss of you, fawning over you. That is why they bore you."

"I feel you are being uncomfortably perceptive," the Marquis remarked.

"It is true, is it not?" Shikara asked. "I can see you are very rich, and of course as you also have a title women run after you like a lot of hungry dogs. It is really rather horrifying when you think about it. They do not want you . . . they want what you possess."

"You are too young to be such a cynic," the Marquis remarked.

"I am not really a cynic," Shikara replied. "I am just truthful and very few people speak the truth. Papa says it gets them into a lot of trouble, but then he is talking about things that happened centuries ago and he has only a few people to argue with him about that. Everything I say causes an immediate argument with everyone round me."

"If you are always as frank with them as you are with me," the Marquis said dryly, "I am not surprised!"

"I am sorry if I have offended you," Shikara apologised. "After all, I should be grateful for your looking after me, and I am certainly very grateful to you for taking me to the station."

She glanced at the clock as she spoke.

"Ought we not to be getting ready?"

"There is no hurry," the Marquis answered, "and quite frankly, what concerns me is the fact that you will get very cold without a cloak."

He rang the bell as he spoke and instantly a footman appeared.

"Ask Hignet if we have anything in the house in the way of a cloak or wrap for the young lady," he said. "Perhaps Lady Sarah left something the last time she was staying here."

"I'll enquire, M'Lord."

"Who is Lady Sarah?" Shikara asked curiously.

"My sister," the Marquis replied. "She is married and lives in the country and when she comes to London she uses this house as if it was an Hotel. She usually leaves a profusion of possessions behind her, some of which we keep until she comes again, many of which have to be conveyed to the country at a great deal of inconvenience and expense!"

Shikara laughed.

"Let us hope your sister has left something really useful behind this time."

Her wish was granted.

A little later Hignet appeared with a cloak in his hands that was of black velvet, lined with sable.

"This is the only thing I can find, M'Lord. Her Ladyship wears it when she goes to the theatre."

"I think that would prove quite adequate," the Marquis said.

Shikara gave a little cry.

"It must be very valuable! Your sister will hardly be pleased at my borrowing it, especially as she may not get it back for some time."

"I think we will risk her wrath," the Marquis said. "Think if you died of pneumonia on your way to Egypt how it would lie on my conscience."

"In which case," Shikara said with a little sideways glance at him, "I accept such munificence most gratefully."

It was certainly very becoming when she put it on at the last moment before they left the house.

The Marquis's comfortable carriage, drawn by four horses, was waiting outside and behind it was another carrying Hignet and the luggage.

Shikara's valise went with him and she thought how small and inadequate it looked beside the great pile of trunks which belonged to the Marquis.

She climbed into the first carriage and the Marquis followed her.

It was still dark, but the stars were fading and there was no longer a moon to vie with the glaring gas-lights in the street.

The horses started off at a brisk rate and Shikara leant back against the comfortable cushions of the well-padded carriage.

"This is where my adventure begins," she said in an excited voice, "and I think ... yes, I really think I have escaped! However, I am keeping my fingers crossed, which is always a wise precaution."

"Very wise!" the Marquis said mockingly.

Chapter Two

Sitting in the swaying railway-carriage, Shikara thought with satisfaction that she had evaded her Uncle and was free.

At the same time, she thought that she would not feel really safe until the ship that was to carry her to Egypt had left Southampton.

Hignet had procured her a reserved compartment to herself, which actually was next to the one in which the Marquis was travelling, also alone.

She had been provided with a foot-warmer, a rug, and already she had sampled the hot soup and tea in her hamper, the containers of which were wrapped in flannel.

The carriages on the train were new and they were certainly superior to many of those in which she had travelled with her father in other parts of the world.

At the same time, despite Lady Sarah's fur-lined cape, it was very cold; Shikara felt that the tip of her nose must be blue, and there seemed to be draughts coming in from every part of the carriage.

She had taken off her bonnet before reaching Nine Elms Station and had pulled over her head the hood which was attached to the cape.

The fur framed her small face and fair hair and made her look very alluring, but the Marquis was obviously not interested in her.

"Hignet will see that you have everything you want," he said, and went to his own carriage.

Shikara had in fact tried to pay Hignet twenty shillings, which was the First Class fare to Southampton.

Hignet had shaken his head.

"You are His Lordship's guest, Miss. I am sure he did not intend you to pay for your own ticket."

Shikara tried to insist, then told herself she was being foolish.

She would need every penny she had in her handbag and knew that when she reached Southampton she would have to sell a piece of her mother's jewellery.

The fare on the steam-ship to Alexandria would certainly be expensive and in actual cash she only had a few sovereigns in her purse.

When she was alone in the carriage she opened her valise and took out her jewel-box.

She told herself that she had taken a senseless risk in putting her jewels into her valise, which she had actually left behind on the pavement when she ran away from the Marquis.

Supposing she had never seen it again?

If that had happened she would have been forced to return to her Uncle's house and doubtless would have been punished for her escapade.

She opened the jewel-box and looked with satisfaction at the pearls, diamonds, rubies, and sapphires which reposed inside on beds of velvet.

Some of the jewels, especially the larger diamonds, her mother had inherited.

But her father had been a generous husband, and perhaps because he had a guilty conscience about the times when he left his wife alone or took her on extremely uncomfortable journeys, he had always tried to compensate her with expensive gifts.

Shikara looked at the jewels and thought she could almost name the countries they represented.

The rubies her father had brought back from India, when her mother had stayed at home for her to be born. They were exquisitely set with small diamonds and pearls and backed with a mosaic of enamel in the way that the Indian craftsmen had done for generations for the Rajput Princes.

The pearls Shikara remembered him buying in Persia, the sapphires in Ceylon, and the opals in Turkey.

She did not care for them, believing the British superstition that they were unlucky, but she loved the turquoises that had come from various different parts of the East.

Although they were by no means the most valuable, they were in fact her favourite stones.

"I will sell one of the brooches," she decided.

She picked out a crescent set with large blue-white diamonds, which she was sure would fetch her enough money to last for months.

Because she thought it was safer, she pinned the brooches on the inside of her coat and hung several necklaces round her throat underneath the white lace collar of her blouse.

The bracelets were more difficult because she thought they would show on her wrists, so she wrapped them up in a handkerchief and put them with various other objects in her pocket.

'Now if I lose my valise,' she thought, 'I shall still have my fortune with me."

Then because after moving about and taking off her fur-lined cloak she was shivering, she opened the hamper to eat some of the delicious sandwiches it contained and to drink a little more of the hot tea.

At Woking, which was the first stop, Hignet came along to see if there was anything he could get for her.

"I have everything, thank you," Shikara said with a smile.

"I'm afraid it's very cold, Miss."

"I am very glad of the rug and of course Lady Sarah's cloak."

"You'll soon be warm when you gets to the sun, Miss, and I'm sure we will be beating you to it, so to speak, in His Lordship's new yacht."

Shikara looked interested, and Hignet explained:

"The newest and fastest yacht in Britain at the moment, that's what the *Sea Horse* is. I don't mind telling you, Miss, I'm looking forward to sailing in her."

"I am sure you are," Shikara smiled.

"Well, if there's nothing I can do for you, Miss . . ."

"Nothing, thank you, but when we get to Southampton I should be grateful if you could procure me a hackney-carriage."

"His Lordship told me you'd be going to the docks," Hignet said, "but if there's not a ship in harbour, might I suggest, Miss, you goes to the Royal Cumberland? It's where His Lordship always stays when we have to spend a night in Southampton."

"Thank you. I was going to ask you which would be the best Hotel," Shikara told him.

The guard blew the whistle and Hignet hurriedly shut the carriage door and ran down the platform to his own compartment in the Second Class portion of the train, where he travelled with all the luggage.

"He is a sensible man," Shikara said to herself. "I wish Papa could find someone like that to look after him and, if nothing else, to remind him to write home."

She did not believe her Uncle's contention that her father was dead, though it was in fact very strange that she had not heard from him for so long.

But she knew better than anyone else how engrossed her father could become in any new discovery or new "dig," as the Archaeologists called it.

Then he would seem almost to be transported into the past. He would often go a whole day without food simply because he never thought of himself or had any idea that he was hungry.

Nevertheless, nine months was a very long time for him not to communicate with her, unless of course he was in some obscure and isolated part of the country from which there were no posts.

'Anyway, I will find out for myself,' Shikara thought, 'and I will persuade Papa not to allow me to be married off as Uncle Hardwin wishes.'

She had realised that her Uncle was antagonistic towards her from the first moment she had gone to live with him.

He liked quiet, mousy little women who agreed with every word he said, and had brow-beaten his wife into a state where she would never have dared to express an opinion that was contrary to his.

Shikara, who was used to arguing with her father and discussing subjects about which her Uncle had no knowledge whatsoever, could not bring herself to be the inarticulate, witless creature he desired.

He had therefore tried to crush and subdue her by every means in his power, and had only just stopped short of physical violence although he had at times come perilously near to striking her.

She thought it would give him tremendous satisfaction to carry out his threat of beating her on the grounds that she would not obey him and marry Lord Stroud.

That Lord Stroud had offered for her had in fact taken Shikara by surprise.

He had often been in the house, but that was because he was a friend of her Uncle's; and although he seemed to seek out her company at Receptions and had several times at Balls offered to take her in to supper, she had never for a moment thought of him as a suitor.

In fact, she was convinced he was interested in no-one but himself.

She had therefore been astonished when her Uncle had called her into his Study and informed her that Lord Stroud had asked for her hand in marriage and that he had given his consent to the union.

"Marry Lord Stroud?" Shikara had said in astonishment. "I would not marry him if he were the last man on earth!"

"You will marry him," her Uncle had retorted, "because he is the right type of husband to keep you in order and curb your flighty and irresponsible nature. What is more, he has a position and title which any woman would be proud to share."

"Any woman but me!" Shikara had replied. "I am not interested in titles, and I certainly do not wish to marry a man who is almost old enough to be my grandfather!"

She had seen the fury in her uncle's face. Immediately they were shouting at each other, Shikara defying Sir Hardwin with a violence that hid effectively her very real sense of fear.

She had not lived for a year in her uncle's house without realising he was a martinet and so determined to have his own way that it was very hard for anyone to withstand the pressure he would bring upon them.

There was no doubt, she discovered, he had made up his mind irrevocably that she would accept Lord Stroud as her husband.

She wondered what he would do when he was informed that she had left the house and the rope was found dangling from her bed-room window.

Then, feeling nervous that he might at the very last moment prevent her from leaving the country, she looked at the clock which she carried in her valise not once but a dozen times in the next hour.

The train seemed to be travelling slower as they got towards Southampton, and looking out the window Shikara realised it was because there was a fog or a sea-mist.

She was not certain which it was but it made it almost impossible to see beyond a few yards down the railway track.

At first she felt frantic at the thought of the delay.

Then she told herself sensibly that if she could

not reach Southampton, then her uncle, if he was in pursuit of her, would not be able to get there any quicker.

Nevertheless, it was with a great sense of relief that she found that the train was gliding into the station, although it was in fact an hour late.

Hignet, who came to help her from the carriage, had already engaged a porter to carry her valise.

"If you go to the entrance, Miss," he said respectfully, "I'll just see to His Lordship before I join you,"

"Thank you," Shikara answered.

She realised as she stepped onto the platform that the Marquis had already alighted. He looked exceedingly elegant in a thick travelling-cloak, his hat set on his dark head at an angle which most women found attractively raffish.

But Shikara was thinking only of her own difficulties and she realised as she reached his side that there was a slight scowl on his face as he looked at her.

"There is no chance, I suppose, of your having second thoughts and deciding to return to London?" he asked.

"None at all," Shikara answered.

"In which case I must wish you *bon voyage*, Miss Bartlett, and hope when you reach Egypt you will find your father in good health."

"Thank you very much ... thank you too for bringing me as far as this. I am very grateful to you."

"I have told Hignet to find you a hackney-carriage at once," the Marquis said. "Then he can return to collect my luggage."

He looked, Shikara thought, rather disparagingly at her valise, which the porter was carrying.

"Again I can only say thank you," she said, dropping him a curtsey.

He raised his hat as she walked away to find at the entrance to the station that Hignet with his usual efficiency had a hackney-cab waiting for her.

"I've told him to go to the Royal Cumberland, Miss," he said as he helped Shikara in.

As she reached for her purse, he added:

"I'll tip the porter, Miss. I hope you have a good journey."

"Thank you, Hignet."

She smiled at the efficient little man. As the carriage moved away she felt almost as if she were leaving a friend behind.

"Now I really am on my own," she told herself.

As soon as they were clear of the station she knocked to alert the driver and tell him that she wished to go first to the best jewellers in the town.

❖   ❖   ❖

The Marquis drove to the harbour, leaving Hignet to follow in another carriage with the luggage.

He had instructed the Captain of his yacht to be ready to sail at any time he required—it was one of the conditions under which the Captain had been engaged.

Now as he saw the *Sea Horse* he noted with pleasure that it looked ready to put out to sea as soon as the mist lifted.

It was, however, still very thick round the harbour itself, and the Marquis, having stepped aboard and greeted the Captain and told him of his plans, drove back into the town to purchase books, newspapers, and magazines that he thought he might need on the voyage.

As the yacht was new, he had not had time to accumulate the considerable Library which he always took with him when he went to sea.

He enjoyed reading but found that when he was in London and even in the country there were so many other things to do that he had little time for books.

A sea voyage was a perfect time in which to "replenish his brain" and he was pleased to find that there were on sale at the local book-shop a number of books he had for some time intended to read.

He noted when he came from the shop that the mist, far from rising, appeared to be thicker than ever.

'What we need is a wind,' he thought.

Then his nautical experience came to his aid and he thought it would be likely to start to blow with the turn of the tide.

The carriage he had hired drove very slowly back to the harbour, and while his purchases were being carried on board, the Marquis had a closer look at the *Sea Horse*.

Early this year the Peninsular and Oriental Line had launched the *Himalaya*, the new ship being an iron-screw steamer which caused all other ships to appear out-of-date.

The Marquis had with considerable courage decided two years ago to have a yacht of the iron-screw type.

He had seen the screw-propellor which had been introduced by the Inman Line into the European-Atlantic companies.

The first of these ships had been iron-screw steamers of less than two thousand tons, barque-rigged and still maintaining a full spread of canvas.

This example was soon followed by the Germans and the French, but the English, who had endeavoured to carry on in their traditional way, were finally forced into line and produced the *Himalaya*, which at 3,438 tons was the largest vessel of its type in the world.

The Marquis had ordered the *Sea Horse* to be built in the same ship-yard.

It was very large for a private vessel, but he considered it well worth the expense and he expected that when he took her to Cowes in the Isle of Wight for the yacht-racing week she would cause a sensation.

But he was in fact not so interested in impressing his friends and rivals as in travelling in comfort.

He enjoyed the sea and he had done a number of voyages in sailing ships which most men of his class would have found far too arduous and uncomfortable.

'Of one thing I am sure,' the Marquis thought

with a smile, 'neither Hignet nor I will be able to complain of discomfort in this vessel!'

She looked very trim with her gleaming white paint, two high auxiliary masts, and a flag flying at her stern.

Satisfied by the outward appearance of his yacht, the Marquis went aboard and was delighted with his first sight of the Saloon.

He had chosen the colours, the furniture, and the pictures with the same attention to detail that he gave to his houses and horses.

Hignet was smiling as he brought him a glass of champagne, and the Marquis, seating himself in a comfortable chair, raised his glass as he said:

"To our voyage, Hignet, and I think this ship will find us new worlds to conquer!"

"It's bigger than I thought, M'Lord," Hignet replied, "and you seem to have thought of every detail."

"I hope I have," the Marquis answered. "I certainly gave it a lot of serious thought."

He glanced towards one of the port-holes as he spoke.

"When does the Captain think we can sail?"

"When I last enquired, M'Lord, he hoped the mist would lift on the turn of the tide."

That was what the Marquis had thought himself and it was pleasant to know that he had been accurate in his surmise.

"I will go on the bridge and speak to the Captain," he said as he finished his glass of champagne.

This, both he and Hignet knew, was merely an excuse for him to have a further look at the ship.

He had seen it when it was launched, but then the furnishings were not complete, nor was the superstructure.

However well a design had been drawn or the plans executed, there was nothing quite so satisfactory as the finished article.

The Marquis went to the bridge, where he not

only talked to the Captain but was also introduced to several members of the crew.

There were twenty-five in all and their accommodation was much more modern and comfortable than they had encountered on any other ship on which they had served.

They were therefore extremely complimentary about the design of the *Sea Horse.*

"How soon shall we leave, Captain?" the Marquis enquired.

"I am just waiting for some last stores to be brought aboard, My Lord, then I think we will be able to risk taking her slowly out of harbour," the Captain replied. "I know this part of the world like the back of my hand and I am prepared to risk moving, if Your Lordship is."

"The sooner the better as far as I am concerned," the Marquis replied. "But do not pile her up on a rock, Captain!"

This was of course a joke, and the Captain laughed before he replied:

"I am too proud of her to do that, My Lord."

The Marquis went below.

Having taken off his travelling-cloak and hat and given them to Hignet, he settled himself to read the newspapers.

He could not however prevent himself from feeling slightly excited when the engines started up and a little later he felt the ship moving slowly but smoothly out of the harbour.

He threw down the newspapers and once again went up on the bridge.

By the time the yacht was away down Southampton Water, the mist was dispersing and a very pale, fitful January sun had begun to peep through the clouds.

The rest of the day the Marquis spent either on the bridge or in the Saloon, reading first the newspapers, then one of the books he had bought in Southampton.

However, he could not help his thoughts continually going back to what had happened the night before and wondering what Lord Shangarry had thought when he visited his house in Grosvenor Square only to find that his prey had disappeared.

The Marquis could imagine with pleasure the chagrin of Shangarry's expression and the anger he must have felt at knowing that his hopes of a large cash settlement had disappeared like a pipe-dream.

At the same time, he continued to feel incensed at the thought of how Inez Shangarry had deceived him.

He was bound to admit to himself in all frankness that he had believed her protestations of affection and thought that unless she was a very much better actress than seemed possible, she had in fact been genuinely aroused by him physically.

Yet all the time she had been plotting with her husband against him.

It was something, the Marquis thought, he would never forgive and would find hard to forget.

Of all the women who had pursued him and whom he had cast aside without a thought when he was tired of them, none of them had really shown themselves to be vengeful, nor as far as he knew actively hated him.

But Inez Shangarry had been devious. She had undoubtedly enjoyed his love-making. No woman could have acted that part so well. Yet at the same time she had been prepared to intrigue with her husband to bleed him white.

"Damn them!" the Marquis said angrily to himself. "Why should I go on thinking about them? I have made a fool of myself and I shall take more care in the future."

But he knew that although Inez Shangarry had pricked his pride and lowered his conceit in himself, it would be a long time before he would forget her.

He hardly gave Shikara a second thought.

He had done his best for the girl. He had brought her to Southampton, and doubtless by this time like himself she was on the high seas, setting off towards Egypt with a confidence and self-sufficiency that had something very unfeminine about it.

'That is the modern girl for you,' the Marquis reflected, 'prepared to travel about the world alone, dispense with a man's protective arm, and think herself independent in an almost masculine manner.'

His thoughts continued:

'She will doubtless grow into a mannish sort of female of uncertain age and will end up exploring the desert on a camel or trying to turn the Bedouins into Christians!'

Then as he remembered Shikara's large grey eyes and fragile appearance he laughed at his own fantasy.

'I suppose,' he went on, 'I should really have enquired what ships were sailing and sent Hignet to book a cabin for her.'

Then he told himself it was none of his business and the last thing he wanted was to be connected in any way with an heiress whose disappearance would doubtless cause a scandal.

"I have had my fingers burnt once," the Marquis told himself, "and I am not putting them in the fire again."

During the afternoon he dozed a little and only aroused himself to repair to his large, luxurious cabin to change for dinner.

Hignet had arranged everything to his satisfaction, and in the *Sea Horse* there was a private bathroom attached to his cabin, an innovation which very few private yachts had yet installed.

The Marquis bathed, then dressed as resplendently as if he were going to dine at his Club or with a party of friends, and sat down to an excellent dinner cooked by a Chef whom he had chosen with as much care as he had chosen the Captain.

The Marquis enjoyed food only when it was superlative and he thought with satisfaction that he had seldom tasted lobsters better prepared or quails that were roasted so exactly to his requirements.

There was a large choice of dishes and the Marquis did justice to most of them, while the wine, which came from a well-stocked cellar, was worthy of an epicure.

The two stewards who waited on him were well up on their duties, and he thought as the meal finished that he had been wise in choosing experienced men who had either served aboard one of the well-known Transatlantic Liners or had been in the service of a yacht-owner as fastidious as himself.

The dinner was cleared away and the Marquis had just picked up the book in which he had been engrossed earlier in the day when Hignet entered the Saloon.

"Excuse me, M'Lord," he said, "but I think I should bring something to Your Lordship's notice."

"What is it?" the Marquis asked.

He saw that Hignet was perturbed and it surprised him because usually the valet was calm and outwardly unruffled whatever happened.

"I'd like to show Your Lordship what I've found, if you'll accompany me," Hignet said.

Curious, the Marquis rose to his feet and Hignet led him from the Saloon down the passage towards his own cabin.

Just before he reached it he opened the door into what the Marquis knew was a guest-cabin.

He had fitted it out extremely attractively. There was a brass bedstead in the centre while the rest of the furniture was of extremely expensive polished rose-wood.

The room appeared to be empty and the Marquis wondered what Hignet wished to show him. Then the valet bent down and raised the damask valance which surrounded the bed.

"Look, M'Lord," he said.

The Marquis did as he was told and saw to his complete astonishment that there was someone lying in the darkness beneath the bed, someone who apparently was fast asleep.

There was no need for him to look closer to know who it was.

He recognised the fair hair lying on a pillow that Shikara must have taken from the bed, and the black velvet fur-lined cloak with which she had covered herself to keep warm.

Her eyes were closed and her lashes were very dark against her white skin. Beside her on the floor, hidden under the bed, was her valise, which the Marquis remembered and also her hand-bag.

He stared at her for a moment, then said sharply:

"Awaken Miss Bartlett, Hignet, and send her to me in the Saloon."

He did not wait for an answer but walked out of the cabin and back to the Saloon with his anger rising with every footstep he took.

How dare this girl behave in such a manner? How dare she come aboard his yacht and thrust herself upon him?

God knows he had given her little enough encouragement, and yet here he was saddled with her!

He supposed the only thing he could do would be to divert the yacht from its intended course and put Shikara ashore at Plymouth or perhaps Cherbourg.

"The impudence of it! The damned impudence of it!" the Marquis raged to himself.

He was scowling ferociously when some minutes later the door of the Saloon opened and Shikara came in.

She was wearing the tightly buttoned jacket in which he had first seen her, but her head was bare and her hair seemed very fair and slightly ruffled round her small face.

Her eyes were large and apprehensive, but she carried her chin high and walked towards the Marquis, who made no effort to rise, but sat waiting until she was opposite him.

"Well?" he asked sharply, as she did not speak. "What have you to say for yourself?"

"I am ... sorry," Shikara replied, "but I ... hoped you would not ... find me so ... soon."

"What has that got to do with it?" the Marquis asked. "Sooner or later you would have been discovered, and let me say I consider it a vast impudence, an intrusion upon my privacy, a complete outrage for you to have come aboard my yacht uninvited!"

"I ... I am sorry," Shikara said again.

The ship gave a little lurch and she reached out to hold on to the table.

"M-may I ... sit down?"

"I suppose so," the Marquis said grudgingly. "Since you seem to have taken it upon yourself to behave in any way you wish, then apparently my consent is not necessary even to extend you the freedom of my yacht."

"I ... had to come," Shikara said. "There was no ... ship sailing for the Mediterranean until the day after tomorrow. By that time ... Uncle Hardwin might easily have ... caught up with me."

"That is not my affair," the Marquis snapped.

"I ... went to the ... Hotel," Shikara said, "but they said they were full up. I think they did not ... want me as I was alone."

The Marquis was silent as he realised he had not thought of that.

He told himself that it was in fact rather remiss of him not to have warned Shikara that no respectable Hotel would accept a woman of her age unaccompanied and with only a small valise.

She had seemed so confident, so sure of herself, that it had never crossed his mind that this was the sort of situation she might encounter.

For a moment he almost blamed himself for not having considered the possibility of her being unable to find accommodation.

Then the thought of her thrusting herself upon him brought the anger back into his eyes.

"I said you should go home and stop behaving in this ridiculous manner. If you were so intent upon getting away from England you could have taken a steamer to France."

He felt as if he had scored off her by suggesting an alternative action to the one she had taken. Then almost humbly Shikara said:

"I did ... not have ... enough money."

"Are you telling me that you set off on this mad escapade without even considering what it would cost?" the Marquis thundered.

"No ... of course not," Shikara answered. "I obviously had not enough cash available, but I thought it would be easy to sell my mother's jewellery. However, when I went to the jewellers they refused to buy the brooch I offered them. I think they ... thought I had ... stolen it."

The Marquis got to his feet to walk across the Saloon as if only by moving could he control the irritation he felt.

"I have never heard such a story of bungling incompetence," he stormed. "Having got yourself in such a mess, why should you expect me to pull you out of it? That is what you are asking, is it not?"

He almost shouted the words at her, and after a moment's pause Shikara said:

"I ... it was ... rather frightening ... not knowing what to ... do, and a ... man spoke to me."

"I told you that was the sort of danger any girl might expect walking about the streets alone," the Marquis replied.

"And so I thought the only way to be . . . safe was to come with ... you," Shikara said. "I will be no ... trouble ... I will keep out of your sight ... in fact you need not even ... know I am on ... board."

"Is that likely?" the Marquis asked. "Anyway, 1 do not intend to carry an unwanted guest. The question is whether I deposit you at Plymouth or at Cherbourg."

There was no answer and after a moment he said sharply:

"Well—which is it to be?"

Shikara clasped her hands together and looked at him, and her eyes were very large and pleading.

"Please... take me a little further. If you leave me at ... Cherbourg I shall have to go overland to Marseilles. I did that journey once with Papa and it was very... uncomfortable... and I think I might be ... frightened alone."

"It would be a very good thing if you were! It would perhaps make you see sense and go back to your Uncle."

"And m-marry Lord Stroud?" Shikara asked. "Never!"

"You cannot go wandering about the world without money, and as I told you before you have no idea of the dangers which could be waiting for you."

"I am ... beginning to understand them," Shikara said. "The m-man who ... spoke to me in the street was... horrid! I ran away... but I thought he might... follow me."

"God!" the Marquis exclaimed. "Was any man more bedevilled by women than I? Why should I have to put up with all this ridiculous play-acting? You are not my responsibility. I never even saw you before last night, and when we reached Southampton I hoped and expected to see the last of you."

"Neither had I any wish to see you again!" Shikara retorted, as if the words were forced from her lips. "If you think I am running after you because of your attractions you are very much mistaken! I hid in your yacht simply because I was afraid that Uncle Hardwin might be looking for me! I had no other reason, and if you are apprehensive—do not flatter yourself that I have designs upon you!"

She spoke so rudely that the Marquis stared at her in surprise. Then because he was reminded once again of a small tiger-cub at the Zoo he laughed.

"Well, at least we are being frank with each

other," he said, and found to his surprise that his anger had abated.

He sat down again on the chair he had vacated.

"We must talk this over sensibly, and as I know you have had no dinner, and I very much suspect no luncheon either, I suppose I should ask the steward to bring you some food."

"After all you have said to me I think it would stick in my throat!" Shikara answered.

"I doubt it," the Marquis replied dryly. "In the meantime, let me offer you a glass of champagne. I feel that after all you have experienced you need one."

He rose again to go to the corner of the Saloon where there was an open bottle of champagne resting in an ice-cooler that was firmly fixed to the floor, where it could not move with the roll of the ship.

The Marquis poured some of the wine into a cut-crystal glass and gave it to Shikara. Then he rang the bell to summon the steward.

"Now you are being nice to me, and I am becoming suspicious," she said. "Are you intending to throw me overboard?"

The Marquis laughed—he could not help it.

"It is certainly an idea," he said, "a solution that actually had not come into my mind."

"I have always thought the sea was the easiest way of disposing of anything one did not want," Shikara said.

"Can you swim?" the Marquis enquired.

Shikara nodded.

"I might have suspected it!" he said. "Then you would swim ashore or perhaps ride on a dolphin's back, and give evidence against me. I half-suspect you of being a witch, turning up on your broomstick at the most inconvenient moment."

Before Shikara could answer, the steward stood in the doorway.

"Ask the Chef to provide dinner for a young lady who is extremely hungry," the Marquis said, "and tell the Captain I wish to speak to him."

As he spoke he saw the expression on Shikara's face. Just for a moment he hesitated, then before the steward had left the cabin he added:

"Do not trouble the Captain. I will see him my-self later."

As the door shut Shikara bent forward to say:

"Please take me ... further than Cherbourg. I swear I will be no ... trouble."

"Trouble?" the Marquis ejaculated. "You have been nothing but trouble since the first moment I saw you."

"I know," Shikara agreed, "but it is not my fault ... it is not ... really."

"That may be a matter of opinion," the Marquis answered. "But let me make it quite clear—I am not intending to go as far as Alexandria."

"You could put me ashore at Gibraltar," Shikara suggested. "I stopped there twice when I was with Papa. The last time was when I was ten, but I do not suppose it has changed much."

It came to the Marquis's mind that she would have been far safer in Gibraltar when she was ten, considering all the garrisons stationed there, than at eighteen.

However, aloud he merely remarked:

"I will think about it."

There was silence and after a moment Shikara said:

"You are not still as ... angry as you ... were, are you?"

"I was very angry when I saw you—very angry indeed. In fact if I was not extremely civilised, and I might almost add a Christian man, I might have thrown you overboard, which is what you deserve."

She laughed and for the first time he noticed that she had a dimple on one side of her mouth.

"I have a feeling that you are the sort of man who thinks first and acts afterwards," she said. "I am the opposite. I act first, then think afterwards."

"That I might have guessed!" the Marquis said sarcastically.

"I hope you do not think I regret running away," Shikara said. "I am glad ... very glad to have escaped from Uncle Hardwin ... and whatever happens to me ... however difficult it might be ... I will not go ... back."

"I suppose you realise that when what money you obtain for your jewellery runs out you will have to notify him if you want any more," the Marquis said. "He doubtless has the handling of your fortune and can refuse to give you a penny unless you return."

"My jewellery will last for many months, but if I do not find Papa in time, I will work and earn some money of my own."

"It sounds very ambitious," the Marquis said cynically, "and what work do you think you are capable of doing?"

"Oh ... I will find some sort of employment once I get to Egypt," Shikara replied. "I can speak Arabic for one thing."

"You can?"

"Of course! I was always having to help Papa by writing letters for him to the authorities. I know quite a number of languages, as it happens, some of them not very well, like Turkish, which I found very difficult. But Persian was easy and Arabic I have been able to speak ever since I was a baby."

"I am still more surprised!" the Marquis remarked.

"Just because you hate women does not mean to say that we are all empty-headed fools," Shikara retorted. "Perhaps you have met the wrong sort of women!"

The Marquis thought this might easily be true, but he merely said:

"What do you call the wrong sort?"

"The type who run after men, flatter and pander to them," Shikara said scathingly.

He laughed.

By the time Shikara had finished dinner he had found himself laughing a remarkable number of times at the things she said.

She might be irritating, and he was quite convinced that as far as he was concerned she was little else, but she undoubtedly had an original way of looking at life and of speaking her mind in a manner that he had never before encountered in a woman.

He was of course used to women who set themselves out to amuse and entertain, which involved using every possible feminine allure while keeping the conversation almost entirely upon themselves.

It was, the Marquis thought, refreshing and at the same time slightly challenging to be with a young woman who told him quite frankly she disliked him as a man.

And yet she appeared to trust herself in his hands apparently without a second thought.

When the meal was cleared away the Marquis sat back with a glass of brandy in his hand and said:

"Now we have to make up our minds about you. If I agree to take you a little farther, will you give me your solemn word of honour that you will not make a scene when finally I deposit you ashore?"

"You ought to know that a woman's word of honour is never the same as a man's," Shikara flashed.

"What do you mean by that?" the Marquis enquired.

"Women do not have to behave like gentlemen," Shikara answered. "For one thing, they do not have to pay their card debts for fear of being ostracised in their Club—they can listen at key-holes—read other people's letters without being shot at dawn, or whatever men do to each other in those circumstances."

The Marquis found himself laughing again.

"Then, if you do not acknowledge my code of honour—what is yours?"

Shikara thought for a moment.

"I would never hurt anyone who had not hurt me ... not intentionally at any rate. I would never say things behind people's backs that I would not say to their faces, and I would not, unless it was impossible not to, lie!"

"Then what are you prepared to swear on?"

She gave him an impudent little look out of the corner of her eyes.

"Cross my heart and hope to die!"

"I do not consider that serious enough," the Marquis answered.

"Oh, but it is very serious," Shikara argued. "I have no wish to die, not yet! There are so many things I want to do in the world."

"Very well," the Marquis conceded, "cross you heart and hope to die that you will not make a scene when I put you ashore."

Shikara put her head on one side.

"I think that is ambiguous. Supposing you choose Devil's Island or some deserted spot in the Pacific where there is nothing but snakes and monster crabs?"

"That is certainly another idea I had not considered," the Marquis answered. "After a year or so in such a place you might even welcome a man, whatever he was like."

"I suppose that is true," Shikara agreed, "but have you ever thought how you would manage in a world without women? After all, you have to face the fact that there would be nobody to admire you except yourself."

There was such a mischievous gleam in her eye that the Marquis said quickly:

"If you talk to me like that I shall very likely emulate you Uncle and beat you."

"I doubt if you would do anything so drastic," Shikara answered. "You would think about it first and decide that you would not wish to appear undignified, or that it would ruffle the elegance of your exquisitely tailored coat!"

"I think that as you were up all last night," the Marquis said, "the sooner you now go to bed the better, and let me point out to you, Miss Bartlett, that you said you would keep out of my way as much as possible and not be any trouble on this voyage!"

He paused to add firmly:

"We will have meals together, but the rest of the time I suggest you leave me to my own devices. I have plenty of things I wish to do, and I think it might be good for you to reflect on the very serious step you are taking."

"Of course I have no alternative but to agree to that," Shikara answered, "except for the bit about reflection. Unless you lend me some of your books, I shall have nothing to do but think about myself, and that would be terribly boring."

"You may help yourself," the Marquis conceded, "and doubtless, when you have finished reading the one you have chosen, Hignet will change it for another if our Library does not run out too soon."

Shikara walked towards the table that he indicated, on which lay the books he had purchased in Southampton before coming aboard.

She looked at them, picking up one, then another, while he watched her.

"They are nearly all of them abour war," she said. "I suppose men like to read about fights when they are not actually engaged in one."

"What did you expect—love-stories?" the Marquis enquired.

"No, I did not!" Shikara replied. "And that is certainly a point to you! I will take this one."

She held up what the Marquis had thought might prove to be a rather dull book concerning the Russian ambitions in Afghanistan.

"Do you think that will interest you?" he asked in some surprise.

"Afghanistan is a place I have always intended to visit," Shikara said quite seriously. "I think I can persuade Papa to go there, once I have found him... that is, if he is not... dead."

There was a note in her voice that made the Marquis think this was a very real fear at the back of her mind.

Then before he could think of anything to say which might perhaps reassure her and give her hope, she walked towards the door, and turned when she reached it and curtseyed.

"Cross my heart and hope to die! I will be as little nuisance as possible," she said. "Try not to think about me. Hating someone always gives one indigestion!"

She vanished and the door shut behind her before the Marquis could think of a suitable retort. Rather ruefully he found himself laughing again.

Chapter Three

For the first three days Shikara kept to the arrangement they had made.

She appeared at luncheon and dinner, and as soon as the meal was over she curtseyed to the Marquis and returned to her own cabin.

Hignet had found her a place up on deck which was out of the wind and where she could sit without getting in the Marquis's way or even being seen by him.

At mealtimes she was witty and provocative, and the Marquis, when he went to bed, found himself remembering some of the things she had said and being amused by them.

He could not remember ever before arguing so fiercely with a woman on abstract subjects.

He found himself continually in disagreement with her; for instance, when she maintained that women should be allowed to do things without being sponsored or patronised by a man, or that when it came to earning her own living she should be paid the same wages.

"You will never find any employer who will agree to that," the Marquis said scornfully. "No woman is as good a workman as a man."

"Surely it depends on the type of work they are doing?" Shikara questioned. "Women work in the cotton-factories and although I believe their produc-

53

tion from the looms is exactly the same as when they are operated by men, their wages are a quarter of what the 'superior sex' earns. It is not fair!"

"Women are employed because they are cheap," the Marquis said firmly. "If they proved to be as expensive as men they would never get employment."

If he tried to think of arguments to answer her assertions, Shikara for her part spent a great deal of time when she was not with him thinking up subjects with which she could defy him.

She enjoyed the cut and thrust of debate in a way that she had not been able to enjoy anything for a very long time.

Being with the Marquis was very different from having to listen to her Uncle lay down the law and allow no-one else to voice an opinion.

She realised that the Marquis was an extremely intelligent man. What was more, his knowledge was far wider than she had expected in a man who was an outstanding social figure.

Her experience with the men she had met at the Balls to which her Aunt had taken her, and with those who were entertained in her Uncle's house, had made her believe that all gentlemen were concerned with nothing but sport, gambling in some form or another, and gossip.

Ever since childhood she had listened to men who had steeped themselves in the study of history, and because of her father's prominence in the Archaeological world they had been entertained in every country they visited by Statesmen, historians, and writers, all of whom Shikara had listened to with interest.

They had travelled so much that her formal education had in fact been patchy.

"My arithmetic is lamentable!" she told the Marquis frankly, "unless I am dealing in local currency, and I soon become an expert in that! Mama always used to say that I had none of the graces."

"What did your mother mean by that?" the Marquis enquired. "Without hearing what they are, I am quite prepared to agree she was right."

Shikara made a little grimace at him before she answered:

"Mama was brought up to believe that every woman should play the piano and be prepared to do so after a dinner-party at home. She should also sew, paint in water-colours, and be able to arrange flowers."

"And can you do none of those things?" the Marquis asked.

"Frankly I do not think you would enjoy hearing me play the piano," Shikara answered. "I loathe water-colours even when somebody else paints them. And I would far rather see flowers growing than stick them stiffly out of vases."

"And what about sewing?" the Marquis enquired.

"I can do that reasonably well," Shikara replied, "but I cannot say I find it enjoyable."

The Marquis shook his head.

"I can quite see you are a hopeless case. We shall never get you married."

"You can be quite sure of that," Shikara retorted. "I have no desire to be any man's wife and be treated as if I were a puppet which would not move unless he pulled the strings."

"You might find a man stupid enough to treat you as an equal," the Marquis said provocatively.

"Meaning he would condescend to me," Shikara said. "I can assure you I do not want to be patronised by anyone, least of all one of your sex."

"I thought at first you were like a tiger-cub," the Marquis told her, "but I can see now I was mistaken. You are really a porcupine, bristling with pointed quills all over your back!"

"I think I prefer being a porcupine to the way Uncle Hardwin used to describe me."

"What did he say?"

"Like most men, he much preferred horses to women, and he continually referred to me as an 'unbroken filly.' "

"I think he had a point there," the Marquis said.

Shikara's eyes flashed in anger, then she laughed.

"You are deliberately trying to make me angry! If I really were a tiger-cub, I would doubtless bite you!"

The interchange of repartee was however interspersed with entirely serious conversation on Eastern religions, on the many excavations in which her father had been interested, and on speculation as to whether anyone would ever discover the source of the White Nile.

"Have you ever been up the Nile?" Shikara enquired.

The Marquis shook his head.

"I have always intended to visit Cairo," he said, "but as it happens I seem never to have had the time."

Shikara looked at him, and he knew what she was thinking.

"If you are suggesting that this is an excellent opportunity for me to do so," he said, "forget it. I have every intention of going to Algiers. I have a friend there whom I have not seen for many years."

"And you will take me as far as that?"

"It depends upon your behaviour," the Marquis replied. "Otherwise I might drop you off at Oporto, or, as you suggested, Gibraltar."

"I will be very, very ... good," Shikara promised. Then as luncheon was finished she rose to leave the cabin.

She was certainly being little trouble, the Marquis told himself, and although he hated to admit it he rather enjoyed having someone to talk to at mealtimes.

What was more, she appreciated the food that his Chef produced with a culinary knowledge and an appetite that he had not encountered before in any woman in whom he had been interested.

Owing to their desire to have small waists, they were usually so tightly laced they were unable to enjoy the large meals that he himself ate.

And although the older women in Society were very experienced hostesses and undoubtedly instructed their Chefs on what to provide, that was not true of the younger, more frivolous ones.

The Marquis had thought that much of the food that he ate in the houses he visited was dull and at times inedible.

He knew that he himself was the exception not in enjoying the lavish table which was to be found in all large houses, but in insisting that any dish served on his own should be prepared with exceptional skill.

"I want quality, not quantity!" he said continually.

'Shikara is certainly an original little creature,' the Marquis thought, then dismissed her from his mind as he went to the bridge to talk to the Captain.

"I'm afraid we are going to run into bad weather, My Lord," the Captain informed him.

"I rather expected the Bay of Biscay to be turbulent at this time of the year," the Marquis remarked.

"It looks as if we might have a gale."

"In which case I am quite certain the *Sea Horse* will stand up to it."

"Of course, My Lord. I was not doubting that," the Captain agreed. "But a real gale at this time of the year can be very unpleasant, and we have a lady aboard."

The Marquis nearly replied that he was not concerned with Shikara's feelings and if she was unwell it would merely serve her right.

At the same time, he woke up the next morning to find that the Captain's prediction was only too accurate.

The sea was whipped by a wind blowing with gale force from the north, which made it extremely rough, and it was almost impossible to keep warm.

Although the *Sea Horse* was larger than most

yachts, even one the size of the *Himalaya* would have been uncomfortable in the roughness of the seas they now encountered.

The yacht certainly pitched and tossed and rolled in a manner which made it extremely difficult to move about and quite out of the question for any food to be prepared.

Hignet brought the Marquis sandwiches at luncheon-time, carrying them not on a plate, because he was an old hand at dealing with storms at sea, but in a basket so that they would not upset as he struggled down the gangways.

The Marquis ate his sandwiches, drank a glass of champagne, and as there was no sign of Shikara went back to the bridge.

He found it fascinating to feel that his yacht was pitting itself against the elements. He was well aware that a great number of small ships and merchantmen perished every year in the Bay.

But when the great waves broke over the bow of the *Sea Horse* he thought with elation that he had in fact built a really first class sea-going ship and that however bad the storm might be they would come through unscathed.

When Shikara did not appear at dinner-time he asked Hignet if Miss Bartlett was all right.

"I think so, M'Lord," Hignet answered. "I knocked on her door about two hours ago and asked if she would like anything to eat. She told me she was quite all right and required nothing."

"She had no luncheon?" the Marquis enquired.

"No, M'Lord. I asked the young lady if she would like anything to eat, but she said no."

"I expect she is feeling sea-sick," the Marquis said with a smile. "It is hardly surprising. The Captain tells me that several of the crew are totally incapacitated."

"You're fortunate, M'Lord, in the way the sea never affects you," Hignet remarked.

"Nor you," the Marquis answered.

The dinner had been slightly varied from what he

had eaten at luncheon, but it was obviously impossible
for the Chef to cook in the galley and therefore everything that was brought to him was cold.

"I think we shall soon be out of this. At any rate
the wind will drop by tomorrow," the Marquis said.

"One advantage in having such a fast ship,
M'Lord," Hignet answered, "is that we shall take less
time passing through the Bay than we have taken on
other occasions."

"That is true," the Marquis said with satisfaction.

When he was alone he picked up a book; but with
the ship doing its best to stand on its head or roll over
on its side the Marquis decided he might as well go to
bed.

He walked down the passage and when he came
to the door of Shikara's cabin he hesitated.

If she was sea-sick, as he suspected, she had not
appealed for help or even asked for a glass of brandy,
which he usually prescribed in such circumstances.

After hesitating a moment the Marquis knocked
at her door.

There was no answer and after waiting he turned
the handle very softly, thinking she might be asleep.

One glance at the bed showed him that it was
empty. Then he saw Shikara lying curled up on the
floor, her hands over her face.

For a moment he thought that perhaps she had
injured herself, and having broken a leg or an arm
was unconscious.

Then as he walked with difficulty towards her,
he realised that while her hands covered her face her
whole body was trembling.

"What is the matter?" he enquired.

He knelt down on one knee beside her and
turned her over to see her face.

"What is wrong?" he asked. "Are you ill?"

She moved her hands and now her eyes looked up
at him. They were very dark, the pupils dilated in a
very white face.

For a moment he stared at her, then he said in astonishment:

"You are frightened!"

Shikara made a convulsive murmur, then scrambling onto her knees flung herself at him and hid her face in his shoulder.

The Marquis's arms went round her automatically and he sat down on the floor, holding her against him.

He could feel her trembling, and he realised she was not dressed but was wearing only a nightgown.

Her body was very slim and immature, and she was trembling in a manner which the Marquis had never previously encountered.

"It is all right," he said soothingly.

"Are . . . we going to the . . . bottom?"

He could hardly hear the words as they were spoken against his coat.

"I can promise you that if we do," he said, "I shall ask for my money back. The *Sea Horse* was guaranteed as being sea-worthy!"

He hoped as he spoke that the laughter in his voice would reassure her.

She did not seem to tremble so violently, but she did not move and her face was still hidden.

"I . . . I am . . . afraid," she said after a moment. "I cannot . . . help it. I have . . . always been afraid in a . . . storm."

"That is quite understandable," the Marquis said, "and this is a particularly unpleasant variety. At the same time, Shikara, I can assure you we shall weather it, if that is the right word, and the Captain thinks that by tomorrow the wind will be dropping."

He realised as he spoke that she was holding on to the lapel of his coat in a grip that was almost frantic. Now her fingers loosened slightly and he felt a little sigh of relief run through her.

"I am . . . ashamed," she said after a moment.

"It is quite understandable in—a woman!" the Marquis replied.

There was a pause before the last two words and

Shikara made a little choked sound that was almost a laugh.

"Of course," the Marquis went on, "I am delighted to find that under that aggressive, independent exterior you have in fact a distinctly feminine streak. You are afraid, Shikara, and at the moment you are clinging to me exactly as any normal woman would cling in the circumstances."

He felt her whole body stiffen, then she looked up at him to say:

"Th . . . that is not . . . cricket . . . you are . . . hitting below the belt!"

"I am certainly not behaving as a gentleman should," the Marquis answered, "but you have told me so often that you want to be on equal terms with a man."

Shikara made an effort as if she would move away from him, but at that moment the ship gave a violent lurch which seemed to make the whole vessel shake and rattle.

With a little murmur she put her face back against the Marquis and her fingers closed tightly on his lapel.

The Marquis smiled. Then he said:

"I think you are feeling things are worse than they really are, simply because you have had nothing to eat or drink. I am going to help you into bed, Shikara. Then I am going to insist that you have something to eat and a glass of champagne to drink, if Hignet can possibly carry it here."

"It is . . . too . . . too much trouble," Shikara whispered.

He knew she was making an effort to reply to the matter-of-fact tone of his voice.

"I was always taught that nothing is too much trouble where a woman is concerned," the Marquis remarked. "After this, Shikara, I shall be quite certain that you are a woman and not, may I say, in the least masculine."

With some difficulty he managed to help her to

the bed, and she crept into it to pull the bed-clothes over her, looking up at him with wide and still-frightened eyes.

The Marquis sat down on the mattress facing her.

As he did so he felt her hand clutching his and holding on to him as if he were a life-line which would save her from drowning.

"I am going to ring for Hignet," he said. "He has much more experience than I have at moving about in a storm, and if you would like me to I will stay here with you, Shikara."

"P-please ... stay."

He could hardly hear the words, but her eyes were fixed on his face and he knew what she wanted without words.

It was an hour later before Shikara, having had something to eat and drink, was definitely feeling sleepy.

"If you are afraid in the night," the Marquis said, "you have only to shout loud enough and I shall hear you; or if you ring for Hignet he will come. I promise that neither of us will fail you."

"That's right, Miss," Hignet said. "I'll not undress in case the master wants me. Besides, one or two of the crew have nasty cuts and bruises, and there may be a dozen more for me to attend to before the night's out."

"I forgot to tell you that Hignet is a very experienced nurse," the Marquis said. "I think really he should have been a doctor."

Hignet grinned at the compliment.

"I never travels without my medicine chest," he boasted, "and it's a good thing I brought it on this voyage, M'Lord. I shall have to replenish my bandages and plasters when we get to the next port of call."

"I can always rely on you in an emergency, Hignet," the Marquis said.

The valet withdrew and the Marquis released

Shikara's hand and put it under the bed-clothes, then pulled the sheets up under her chin.

"Go to sleep, Shikara," he said. "It will be better tomorrow, I promise you, and try not to be frightened. I know you do not think much of my opinion on many subjects, but I assure you that in choosing a yacht which will carry us to safety I am in fact unequalled!"

"Thank you for being so ... kind."

There was something very wistful in the words and in the way for the moment her defiant spirit seemed to have left her.

"I ... I am sorry to be such a ... nuisance when I promised I would not be," she added.

"You are being feminine," the Marquis replied. "As I told you before, all women are a damned nuisance—which is why I hate them!"

She knew he was speaking jokingly. At the same time, as he shut the cabin door behind him she thought that what he said was very true.

She had tried to keep her promise and disturb no-one even while she had been so frightened that she wanted to scream.

But her good resolutions had been swept aside, and she had in fact been a considerable nuisance, clinging to him and having to be fed after his dinner had been served.

She could not help feeling that after this he would undoubtedly put her ashore at Gibraltar and not take her on to Algiers, which was what she had hoped.

"It will be my own fault," she said. "I cannot think why I am so ... foolish."

The ship was rolling violently but she did not feel as afraid as she had before. She also felt very sleepy and as her eyes closed she was not quite certain where her thoughts ended and her dreams began.

❋   ❋   ❋

"I gave the young lady something to make her sleep," Hignet was saying to the Marquis as he helped him undress.

"That was sensible," the Marquis replied. "Did you put it in the champagne?"

"Yes, M'Lord. She never noticed it. Few ladies have your palate, M'Lord. I'd never get away with slipping anything unbeknown to Your Lordship."

"Do not let Miss Bartlett hear you," the Marquis said. "She is continually telling me that women are as good as men in almost every particular, except, it appears, in being afraid in a storm."

"There's a good many men as doesn't like it either," Hignet said.

That I can believe," the Marquis agreed. "At the same time, it is natural for a woman to feel afraid, whether of a storm or of a mouse."

"Of course it is, M'Lord," Hignet answered.

When the Marquis was alone he found himself thinking of how convulsively Shikara had trembled in his arms and how slight and light her body was.

He was used to voluptuous, big-breasted women, like Inez Shangarry, and he could not remember when he had last held close anyone as slender as Shikara.

"She is very young," he told himself. "She will get over these ridiculous notions about men and find a husband who will look after her."

He wondered what sort of man would finally attract her.

"He would have to be intelligent," the Marquis told himself.

He thought of their conversations and the extent to which Shikara not only had clearly absorbed the beauty of the places she had visited but also had shown knowledge of the customs and traditions of different nations, which surprised him.

He had always been interested in the history of different countries but seldom had found anyone who shared his interests to any great extent; which was why he preferred to travel alone with Hignet.

He found himself remembering now that he had always intended some day to visit Egypt.

The history of the Pharaohs had fascinated him and he had followed with great interest the discoveries that had been made recently amongst the Pyramids.

"I would like to see the Sphinx," he told himself.

Then he thought he had no intention of pandering to Shikara by taking her up the Nile in his yacht.

'I will go first to Algiers,' he thought. 'Then only if it suits me, I might visit Cairo before I return to England.'

The storm was dying away when the Marquis awoke after having slept well and deeply without having been disturbed.

The *Sea Horse* was still rolling, but the violence of the waves was not to be compared with that of the day before, and when the Marquis went to the bridge the Captain was in good spirits.

"You were right, M'Lord," he said. "The *Sea Horse* is remarkably sea-worthy, and after such a baptism of fire we need never be worried about her again."

"You were worried?" the Marquis asked in surprise.

The Captain looked a trifle embarrassed.

"A new vessel is always a matter for concern, M'Lord, and I have seldom known a worse storm in the Bay, although I have been through it dozens of times."

"You really believed we were in danger?" the Marquis asked.

"I am not ashamed to confess now," the Captain replied, "that I had a few anxious moments."

"It never crossed my mind," the Marquis said truthfully. "You surprise me, Captain!"

"If it would suit Your Lordship I would like if possible to put in to Lisbon," the Captain said. "There are one or two things which should be repaired and the stewards report that quite a lot of crockery has been broken."

"Then we will stop at Lisbon," the Marquis decided.

"Thank you, M'Lord."

The Marquis went down to luncheon to find Shikara already in the Saloon.

She was neatly dressed, but her face was very pale although her eyes lit up when he appeared.

"You are better?" he asked.

"I am perfectly all right," she answered, "and very ashamed of myself."

"There is not the least necessity to apologise."

"I am humiliated that I had not enough will-power to prevent myself from being so stupid."

She saw the Marquis smile and said accusingly:

"Of course, you are delighted! You have proved your point and I am a weak, clinging little woman! What could be more satisfactory from a man's point of view?"

"Shall I say I will not hold it against you?" the Marquis suggested. "We will fight our battles without reference to what occurred last night."

"I suppose you think you are being generous," Shikara said bitterly.

"It is certainly not being accepted in any spirit of generosity," the Marquis retorted.

They sparred with each other over luncheon in the manner to which they had now become accustomed and only when the meal was ended and Shikara would have withdrawn the Marquis said:

"I suggest you stay here in the Saloon this afternoon. You will not disturb me as I am going on the bridge. I dare say after twenty-four hours in your own cabin you are heartily sick of it."

Shikara looked at him a little uncertainly and he added:

"The invitation has no strings! I am not cosseting you or treating you like a weak creature who has no will of her own."

"Very well, I will stay," Shikara said almost defiantly, "but if you find me an encumbrance you have only to say so."

"I assure you I would not hesitate to do so," the Marquis replied.

He left her alone and when he returned two hours later it was to find that she was asleep, stretched out on one of the sofas, her fair hair against a silk cushion.

She looked very young and very fragile and the Marquis sitting down in an adjacent chair looked at her.

What she had been through yesterday had, he knew, been exhausting. There was nothing so unnerving as fear. At the same time, he thought she had a courage that he had not expected to find in a woman, especially in one so young.

'She will get to Cairo and find her father by hook or by crook,' he thought to himself, 'and in defiance of anyone who might try to stop her. She is certainly brave even if she is fool-hardy.'

He picked up a book that he was reading but found it difficult to follow the pages.

His eyes kept wandering towards Shikara and he thought she was in fact very lovely, with a beauty which, when she was not talking or being defiant, had something spiritual about it.

Perhaps it was in the delicacy of her features or in the shape of her face.

He admired her winged eye-brows on either side of a small, straight nose, and he wondered who her mother had been, feeling that such features and her high-instepped little feet could only have come through some aristocratic lineage.

He also wondered what his friends would say if they knew where he was at the moment and with whom.

He could imagine the jokes that would pass round the Club and the remarks which would be made—remarks which he was well aware were always made about him when it was known in whom he was interested.

But it was not the Marquis's fault that his *amours* were so freely discussed.

It was nearly always the woman concerned who flaunted him in the face of her rivals who had been pursuing the Marquis fruitlessly for a long time.

In fact, the Marquis had often been extremely annoyed to discover that people were talking about him long before there were any grounds for it.

'At least,' he thought with satisfaction, 'no-one knows that Shikara is here.'

Once again his thoughts went to Inez Shangarry, and he guessed what she and her husband had said when they found their bird had flown.

He found that both his anger and his sense of humiliation where they were concerned had modified in the last few days.

In a way it was understandable that those who "had not" should wish to take from those who "had," and who was more fortunate than himself in having such an abundance of worldly goods?

He was, however, well aware that it was not only his money which tempted women into indiscretions and into throwing their hearts at his feet.

It was also because he had a certain attraction for them, which he had known ever since he grew to manhood.

"Do you love me?" "Will you love me forever?" "Oh, Osborne, give me your heart."

How often had he heard these phrases repeated again and again, and he could hear, almost as if he were speaking them now, his glib responses, the manner in which he avoided lying while at the same time being reassuring and comforting.

He knew that if he was truthful he had never actually been in love; never had there been any woman to whom he said: "I love you!" with any degree of truth.

"I must be unusual—or perhaps just honest," the Marquis told himself.

At the same time, he was well aware that if he confessed such sentiments to any of his contemporaries they would not believe him.

He remembered the boys with whom he had been at Eton, who had always been frantically in love in their last few terms, usually with an actress or some extremely unsuitable female.

At Oxford it had been exactly the same: half the undergraduates in his year had spent their time not working but pursuing the local girls or members of the Chorus in the plays that appeared at the theatre.

One of his contemporaries at Eton, the Marquis recalled, had been ecstatically and lyrically in love with the wife of one of the Masters.

He would write poems to her and extolled her virtues for hours on end.

"Why have I never been like that?" he asked.

Then he told himself he had no desire to become maudlin over any woman.

Women were there to amuse and entertain. When they ceased to do either, then there was always another woman to take their place.

And what interested a woman except a man? That was exactly how it should be and why the sexes had been created for each other.

Then again he looked at Shikara and thought how extraordinary it was that she should hate men.

"She has been unfortunate in those she has met," the Marquis told himself.

He thought of Lord Stroud and shuddered. He could not imagine that pompous bore kissing and making love to anything so lovely and sensitive as Shikara.

"No wonder she ran away," he said beneath his breath.

As if his thoughts of her aroused her from her sleep, Shikara opened her eyes, saw him sitting on the chair, and smiled sleepily.

"I was ... dreaming of ... you," she said drowsily.

"I am flattered," the Marquis said. "I should have imagined that you would not have allowed a man to intrude into anything so intimate as your dreams."

"We were ... riding over the desert ... I think it was on horses ... but it might have been camels."

"If I have a choice I should prefer a horse," the Marquis said vehemently. "If there is one movement I really dislike it is that of a camel!"

Shikara laughed and woke up completely.

She sat up on the sofa and instinctively her hand went to her hair.

"Am I being a ... nuisance?" she asked. "Shall I retire?"

"I am delighted for you to stay," the Marquis answered. "And have you noticed anything?"

She looked round curiously. Then he said:

"Already the sea is subsiding and is very much smoother that it was."

"Yes, of course," Shikara said. "How wonderful!"

She put her legs to the ground. Then she looked at the Marquis and said in a low voice:

"You were very kind last night. I did not think a ... man could be ... like that."

"Like what?" the Marquis asked.

"Considerate and ... understanding."

"I have come to the conclusion that you have known some very strange types of men," the Marquis said, "just as you think I have known some very odd types of women."

Shikara laughed.

"I can guess what your women have been like," she said. "Brilliant, glittering, and very beautiful. My men have all been incredibly immature and boring, or else old and pompous."

"As I have just said, you have been unfortunate," the Marquis told her. "One day you will meet a man who is different, and then I do not mind betting, Shikara, that you will fall in love."

She looked at him and for a moment their eyes seemed to be held by each other's. Then almost abruptly the Marquis reached out and pulled the bell.

"I suggest that as we are both here together we have English tea—why not?" he asked. "And I am interested to see if my Chef can bake a good cake."

＊　＊　＊

They came into Port Tejo about midday and Shikara watching the yacht moving up the estuary of the Tagus exclaimed at the beauty of the capital of Portugal.

Built on the slopes of a range of small hills above the river's estuary, Lisbon was, the Marquis knew, one of the most spectacular cities in Europe.

"I have always thought," he said as he stood beside Shikara, "that Lisbon rivals Naples and Istanbul in its views and its magnificent setting."

It was certainly very different from most capitals. Round its tiled and multi-coloured buildings was a belt of vines, parks, and woods.

Shikara had already questioned the Marquis about the city and he had told her that the oldest part was Alfama, the eastern district, where narrow, winding streets crowded down to the river between a jungle of trees.

"The central district—Baixa," he went on, "was built in 1755 after an earthquake which laid the place flat. You will find there the streets are broad and there are some excellent shops which I have a feeling you are looking forward to visiting."

Shikara looked at him and asked:

"How can you be so intuitive?"

"Considering the smallness of your valise, I am convinced that you are longing for new clothes."

"Of course I am," Shikara agreed.

It had not escaped the Marquis's notice how skilfully she managed with the few gowns she had with
her.

Being experienced where women were concerned,
he realised that the same white evening-gown had a
number of sashes of different colours and coloured
wreaths with which Shikara rang the changes at dinner.

It was too cold for her to wear anything on deck
in the daytime except her travelling-suit and the magnificent cloak that he had provided for her from his
sister's wardrobe.

But the blouse under her jacket was inter-
changed with one of a different colour and she had
various chiffon scarves which were either draped
round her neck or tied in a soft bow under her small
chin.

Shikara gave a little sigh.

"I would love some new clothes," she said, "but I
do not think it would be wise to spend very much
money on them. After all, as you have pointed out to
me already, when I have sold all Mama's jewellery I
shall have to find employment."

"You told me that would be quite easy."

"I am sure it will be," Shikara said quickly, "but
as I am merely a woman I shall doubtless be unfairly
and sparingly paid!"

The Marquis laughed.

"Very well," he said, "I will be your banker and
give you a loan, to be repaid when you come into
your fortune, or if in the meantime you marry a millionaire."

"I will certainly not marry a millionaire!" Shikara
said, "but . . . "

She paused.

"Well, what is it?" the Marquis asked.

"Mama always said that no lady would take
money from a gentleman."

"You have pointed out to me often enough that

women should be on equal terms with men," the Marquis replied. "If you were a man-friend I would not hesitate to offer you a loan if you needed it, and I am quite certain in the circumstances you would accept it with alacrity."

"If you are quite ... sure it is ... all right," Shikara said doubtfully.

"What do you mean—all right?" the Marquis challenged. "Are you expecting me to dun you for it, or worse still expect some other sort of repayment?"

He spoke without thinking and Shikara looked at him in a puzzled way.

"What could that be?" she asked.

The Marquis realised how innocent the question was and quickly said:

"I might make you work for me. The Chef is already complaining that he wants someone to help with the washing up."

Shikara laughed.

"I would not mind doing that if he taught me to cook as well as he does!"

"You must tell him so," the Marquis said, "he will be flattered."

After some lenghty discussion on how much money she would need they finally went ashore to shop in the broad streets of Baixa, Shikara having twenty-five pounds in her purse.

"You will have to change it into local currency," the Marquis warned, "in which case it will doubtless seem a great deal more."

"What I will need in Egypt," Shikara said reflectively, "will be plenty of thin gowns."

"Yes, of course," the Marquis agreed, "and do not forget to buy a sun-shade and provide yourself with a *topee*. You do not wish to have sun-stroke."

"I have been in far hotter countries than Egypt."

"I apologise if my advice is ill-advised."

"You know I did not mean that," Shikara said. "You have been very kind and I am looking forward

to having a new gown more than I can possibly tell
you. I am heartily sick already of those I have with
me."

"That is a very feminine emotion," the Marquis
said.

But she refused to be drawn into an argument
and merely laughed at him.

The Marquis took her to what was obviously a
very good dressmaker and she was sure would be very
expensive.

There were quite a number of gowns to choose
from and the Marquis was helping her decide, when a
woman coming from one of the fitting-rooms glanced
at him casually, then gave a cry of unmistakable delight.

"Osborne! It is Osborne, not his ghost?" she asked
in a fascinating broken accent. "How could I imagine
that I would see you of all people in Lisbon?"

The Marquis rose to his feet.

"Madalena!" he exclaimed. "This is a pleasure I
did not anticipate. When I last heard you were con-
quering Paris."

"I was a triumphant success there, but after six
months I needed a holiday and so I came home!"

The Marquis kissed her hand, then he said:

"You are even more beautiful than I remember."

That she was beautiful was certainly true, Shikara thought. She had never imagined a woman could
be so glamorous and at the same time have such a
fascinating, alluring face.

As if he suddenly remembered her presence the
Marquis said:

"May I introduce my Ward—Miss Shikara Bartlett?"

As Shikara curtseyed he added:

"*Senhora* Madalena Monteiro is, in case you do
not know, the most famous and the most exquisite
dancer in all Europe."

"You flatter me, Osborne," the *Senhora* said, looking up at him with dark, sparkling eyes which echoed the silky black of her hair.

"You are quite unrivalled," the Marquis insisted, "and you know I am not exaggerating."

"I want to believe you," the *Senhora* smiled. "But tell me, how long are you here? When can I see you?"

"I am afraid we are leaving tomorrow," the Marquis answered, "and that is why you must dine with me tonight, Madalena. I want you to see my yacht. It is new, and like you has no rivals."

"I shall be delighted."

"Will you want to bring any friends?" the Marquis asked.

"You know I want to see you alone," the *Senhora* replied, "so why do you not call for me before dinner so that we can have a tête à tête? Afterwards we can dine on your yacht and I have dozens of friends who would wish to accompany me and meet the most handsome and attractive Englishman I have ever known."

There was something caressing in the way she spoke and the manner in which her hands fluttered towards the Marquis to touch his arm or his chest as she talked.

It made Shikara think that she was like a butterfly, colourful and exotic, fluttering round a flower.

'She is fascinating,' she thought, 'and undoubtedly as overwhelmingly feminine as the Marquis would wish.'

The *Senhora* gave the Marquis her address, and as he kissed her hand she said:

"I shall be counting the hours until tonight, Osborne. It is far too long since we have been together. I shall never forget what a happy time we had in Rome."

"How could I ever forget it?" the Marquis answered. "And you are quite unchanged, Madalena, except that you have grown more beautiful."

The *Senhora* pursed her red lips into the shape of a kiss, then she said softly:

"Until tonight—*au revoir, mon ami.*"

She did not even glance at Shikara as she swept away, the silk of her gown rustling seductively, and the exotic perfume she was wearing lingering on the air after she was gone.

The Marquis returned to the task of helping Shikara choose some gowns.

But she fancied, although it might have been her imagination, that he was no longer so interested and that his thoughts were elsewhere.

Chapter Four

The Marquis was late for dinner.

Shikara, going into the Saloon dressed in one of the new gowns she had bought in the Baixa, found two good-looking elegant Portuguese gentlemen waiting there.

Both of them had high-sounding titles and both immediately started to pay her extravagant compliments, looking at her with large, liquid dark eyes which made her think to herself that they looked like amorous dolphins.

She was rather pleased with the phrase and decided to repeat it to the Marquis when they were alone.

Then as time passed she realised that it was long after the dinner-hour, which had been arranged for half after nine o'clock.

She had been surprised when on their return to the yacht the Marquis told her what time they would dine.

"The Portuguese, like the Spanish, always eat late," he answered. "One has to get used to the difference, although sometimes one's stomach rebels loudly!"

"I know that in Spain luncheon and dinner are very late," Shikara answered. "But I was quite young when we went there and was always sent to bed long before my father and mother had dinner."

"Portugal is much the same," the Marquis told her, "and I have therefore ordered dinner for what to my guests will be an acceptable time."

It was however about seven o'clock when Shikara saw him leave the yacht for the shore.

She had been sitting on deck and without his being aware of it she watched him go down the gangway and get into the boat below.

She thought that in his evening-clothes, with a satin cloak slung over his shoulders, he looked magnificent and unmistakably English.

'Any woman would be proud to be seen with him,' she thought to herself, and wished they were dining alone rather than with a party.

Now she talked with the two Portuguese gentlemen and realised that the time was ticking by without a sign of the Marquis and the *Senhora*.

She wondered if anything untoward had happened to delay them.

Suppose there had been an accident? Suppose that for some unknown reason the Marquis had been detained by the Police or the Military?

As if without words her fear communicated itself to the two guests, one of the Portuguese said:

"Do not be perturbed, Miss Bartlett, I am sure your Chef will realise that we as a nation, and particularly the *Senhora* Madalena, are always late."

"Sometimes with very good reason, especially where Madalena is concerned!" the other gentlemen remarked.

There was a note in his voice which said all too clearly there was an ulterior meaning behind his words.

Shikara looked at him in slight surprise.

Then she realised that the two men had glanced at each other in a manner which made her think they were laughing, if not at her then at some joke she did not understand.

Finally, when it was nearly ten o'clock there was

the sound of activity on deck and Shikara knew the
Marquis and his guest had arrived.

The *Senhora* swept into the cabin looking alluring and breathtakingly glamorous.

Shikara found herself gasping at the amount of
jewellery she wore and the almost outrageous cut of
her gown.

It was very low, very revealing in front, and at
the same time it added to the grace with which the
Senhora walked and the provocative swing of her
hips.

Round her neck and on her arms there was a profusion of emeralds and rubies which few women would
have dared to wear.

Ear-rings of the same stones hung from her ears
and there was a glitter of them in her dark hair.

She held out her hand imperiously to the two
Portuguese gentlemen, who kissed it and went into an
ecstasy of praise at her appearance.

Neither she nor the Marquis made any apology
for being late, and Shikara, looking at the latter,
thought that he seemed to have a more cynical smile
on his lips than usual.

At the same time, she thought, a little despon-
dently that he hardly noticed her or her new gown.

The steward appeared to pour out glasses of
champagne and the three men toasted the *Senhora*,
who smiled beguilingly at all of them.

But she seemed, Shikara thought, to have a spe-
cially intimate exchange of words and glances with
the Marquis, which appeared to set them both apart
from everyone else.

"To your happiness!" the Marquis said, raising his
glass.

The *Senhora* looked at him, her dark eyes slanting mysteriously. Then she said very softly:

"It is you who make me happy—as you well
know."

Shikara thought that the *Senhora* must be declaring her love for the Marquis, then suddenly the truth struck her forcibly, almost like a blow.

How stupid she had been, how obtuse!

Of course the reason why the Marquis and the *Senhora* were late was that they had been "making love"!

Shikara was not quite certain what this entailed, for despite the fact that she had travelled to many parts of the world she was very innocent.

But she knew that a man could make love to a woman without wishing to marry her, and find her desirable without his heart being involved.

That was what had happened! That was why the Marquis having left the yacht at seven o'clock had been away so long, and why the *Senhora* was looking like a cat that had been given an extra dish of cream.

'I should be shocked ... I am shocked!' she thought.

Then she thought that perhaps the Portuguese thought that her position alone on the yacht with the Marquis was in fact open to question.

He had said quite firmly that she was his Ward, but Shikara questioned whether gentlemen of the Marquis's age travelled alone in their yachts or elsewhere with a girl of eighteen.

She had been alone for over three quarters of an hour with the Portuguese and it had never struck her until this second that their compliments might have been more effusive than was suitable to a débutante or that there were innuendos in their conversation that she had not noticed until now.

She felt suddenly embarrassed!

Then she told herself almost bitterly that they certainly need not be concerned about her when it was quite obvious where the Marquis's interests lay and how eagerly his feelings were reciprocated by the *Senhora*.

All through dinner she flirted with him in a manner which Shikara felt would have horrified her mother. Undoubtedly her Uncle would have ordered such a "scarlet woman" out of his house!

At the same time she had to admit that the *Senhora* was fascinating in a way that she had never before realised a woman could be.

Every word she said, every movement she made, seemed to be a calculated enticement to excite a man and to arouse his desires.

And there was no doubt, Shikara thought, watching, that the three men at the table hung upon her words and seemed to be almost mesmerised by her.

"A magnificent theatrical performance!" she told herself, and wondered if in fact the *Senhora* was really enamoured with the Marquis.

Because he was concentrating on someone other than herself and in fact seldom gave her a glance or addressed a word to her, she felt quite unjustifiably piqued.

'He did not invite me to come with him on this voyage, and I have no right to complain,' she thought.

Yet she knew that she felt neglected, although watching the *Senhora* she knew how inadequate she must seem by comparison and was not surprised that the Marquis did not desire her company.

Everyone talked and laughed until the early hours.

Although Shikara would have liked to leave them to go to bed, she felt it would cause a commotion if she rose to her feet.

In fact one of the Portuguese insisted on talking to her in a soft and intimate manner which made it difficult for her to detach herself from him.

She realised he was trying to flirt with her, but it was difficult to listen to him when all the time she was trying to hear what the Marquis was saying.

Finally, when Shikara felt they would never go, the good-byes were begun and she and the Marquis went up on deck to see the guests safely into the boat which was to carry them ashore.

One of the Portuguese gentlemen went first so that he could help the *Senhora*, then before she disembarked she looked up at the Marquis and Shikara heard her say:

"Must you really leave tomorrow?"

"I am afraid I must," the Marquis replied.

"I cannot bear to lose you again, Osborne," she said. "It has been so wonderful being with you, just like old times."

"As you say, like old times," the Marquis repeated.

"Except that you are handsomer, more attractive, and perhaps even more irresistible than you were in the past."

He would have raised her hand to his lips but instead she put her arms round his neck and pulled his head down to hers.

"You will leave a gap in my life which no-one else can fill," she said.

Then her lips met his and the Marquis's arms went round her.

They stood for a moment locked together, and Shikara, watching them wide-eyed, felt a strange sensation within her that was almost like a pain.

She thought it was disgust. Never had she imagined that any woman could have behave so brazenly in public and conduct herself so immodestly.

Then before she could understand her own feelings the *Senhora* and her friends were being rowed away towards the brilliantly lighted shore.

The Marquis turned and walked back to the Saloon and Shikara followed him.

"It is very late," he remarked. "Doubtless we shall both be tired in the morning, having kept the most respectable hours until now."

"Yes ... perhaps we ... will," Shikara answered.

She found it difficult to speak ordinarily but the Marquis seemed not to notice and after a moment he said:

"Good-night, Shikara, I hope you enjoyed this evening. It was a welcome change after the extremities of the storm."

"Good-night ... My Lord."

She curtseyed from the doorway and went to her own cabin.

Only when she was there did she sit down at the dressing-table to stare at her reflection. But all she could see was the attractive, fascinating face of the *Senhora.*

"That is the sort of woman he likes!" she told herself.

The pain in her chest was still there when she thought of how the Marquis had kissed the *Senhora's* lips.

"She is crude and common," Shikara tried to convince herself.

But she knew that in fact the *Senhora* was neither of those things but was a stage personality living in a world of which Shikara had no knowledge.

'What have I to offer the Marquis?' she asked.

She was suddenly appalled at the implication behind the question.

Why should she want to offer him anything? She had told him, as she had told herself so often, that she hated men and wished to have nothing to do with them.

Why then should it matter to her what the Marquis thought or felt about her?

The pain was an agony in her breast, and now because Shikara was honest with herself, as with everyone else, she knew what it was.

It was an emotion she had never experienced before in her whole life, one which she had never dreamt she would ever experience in relation to a man ... it was jealousy!

She was jealous of the *Senhora,* and because she was afraid of asking herself other questions where the Marquis was concerned, she sprang up from the

dressing-table and started to undress almost fever-
ishly.

Only when she got into bed and the cabin was in
darkness did the picture of the Marquis kissing the
Senhora come back to haunt her.

There had been a grace and almost a beauty in
the manner in which they were linked together, their
bodies close against each other's, his head bent to
wards hers, the line of her long neck as she lifted her
mouth to his silhouetted against his evening-clothes.

They looked like the hero and heroine of a ro-
mantic opera and Shikara admitted to herself that it
was a part she herself wanted to play.

The heroine who was admired, fêted, and pursued
by men, the heroine who was finally united with the
hero and kissed as the *Senhora* had been.

Then, horrified by her own thoughts, Shikara sat
up in bed.

Surely she could not be thinking such things?
And yet it was not only her thoughts which had got
out of control: her body was filled with sensations
which she had never before known existed.

It was soft and yielding in a way it had never
been before and her lips trembled because she
wanted to be kissed.

"I must be going mad!" Shikara cried.

When she lay down again, all she could see was
the Marquis, the cynical smile on his lips and the look
in his eyes that had been there when he talked with
the *Senhora*.

'He has never looked at me like that,' Shikara
thought despairingly.

Then she buried her head in her pillow, saying to
herself over and over again:

"What I am feeling cannot be . . . cannot be . . .
love!"

* * *

The yacht began to move out of Port of Tejo at dawn the next morning. When Shikara heard the engines start up she knew with a feeling of intense satisfaction that they were leaving Lisbon and the *Senhora* behind.

She had passed a night of almost intolerable agony, fighting with herself, with her feelings, and inevitably with her mind against what seemed to her to be a new danger.

It was worse than anything she had encountered before.

How could she possibly be in love with a man who hated women? How could she of all people fall in love?

And yet it had happened, and she thought that if the *Senhora* had not been there to make her feel jealous, she might never have been aware of it.

Now she was pulsatingly conscious that the Marquis was sleeping near her and that they were alone in his yacht as they had been before.

The question was, for how long?

'I cannot leave him . . . I cannot!' Shikara thought.

Then she knew she would rather die than let him become aware of what she felt about him.

Now that she was seeing him as an attractive man, she realised that there must have been hundreds of women who had loved him hopelessly but in whom he had no interest.

He had made it very clear that he was not the least concerned with her, and she thought that after all she had said and the way they had argued about her feelings, it would be a tremendous score for him if he realised she was in love.

He would be able to congratulate himself that he had swept away her antagonism towards his sex and made her as maudlinly foolish about him as all the other women he had known in the past.

"He hates me because I am a woman, and yet because he is a kind, considerate person he has to put up with me," Shikara told herself.

She then remembered that the yacht would now not take long to reach Gibraltar!"

She wished that she had never come aboard the *Sea Horse* but had found a steam-ship, as she had intended, to carry her to Cairo.

Then she would never have felt as she did now, and she would have gone on hating men perhaps for the rest of her life.

But regrets did not assuage her feelings toward the Marquis or the fact that when they met at luncheon-time her heart turned over in her breast.

She wondered, as she looked at him, how she had not realised the first moment they had met that he was the most handsome, attractive man that any woman could imagine.

"You slept well?" he asked.

"Very well. thank you," Shikara lied.

"I hope all your purchases came aboard before we sailed," he went on casually. "That is certainly a very becoming gown you are wearing at the moment."

"Thank you," Shikara answered.

But to herself she thought frantically:

'He says that quite automatically and I should be glad that he even notices I am here when his thoughts must be with the *Senhora*.'

Because she could not help her curiosity she asked tentatively:

"Why did you not stay longer in Lisbon? After all, there was really no hurry for you to leave."

The Marquis smiled.

"My old nurse always used to say: 'Enough is as good as a feast!' I have no desire to be caught up in the gaieties with which that city abounds."

Shikara longed to ask him why he did not wish to be with the *Senhora* again, but she was too shy to speak the words that rose to her lips and the Marquis changed the subject.

She felt that he would not wish to discuss anything or any woman who concerned him intimately.

They spoke of other things, but after a while she
could not resist asking:

"Is the *Senhora* Madalena really an outstanding
ballerina?"

"She is indeed exceptional," the Marquis replied,
"and has made a great name for herself in most of the
capitals of Europe."

Shikara longed to ask when they had been in
Rome together, but she felt with sensitive perception
that the Marquis, although he said nothing, was putting a barrier round himself as if as a protection
against her curiosity.

After a moment he said reflectively:

"I suppose really you should not meet actresses or
ballerinas, however famous, but it would have been
impossible for me not to offer my hospitality to an old
friend."

"As your uninvited guest," Shikara answered, "I
am hardly in a position to criticise whoever you ask
me to meet."

"That is true," the Marquis replied. "At the same
time, I suppose I should have remembered that you
are only eighteen and a lady."

"And of course ladies, even if they are women,
can have no fun!" Shikara flashed.

He laughed and they were back into one of their
old arguments.

"Women of your class should be kept immune
from everything that is coarse or ugly in life," the
Marquis said.

"In other words, wrapped in cotton-wool and
kept in a cage," Shikara said fiercely. "I suppose all
men, if they had the choice, would keep their wives in
purdah!"

"It is an excellent idea and one for which I have
always envied the East!" the Marquis replied. "You
can send for a woman when you want her, but other-

wise she is locked away so that she can get into no trouble and certainly not be a disturbing influence."

"That is an autocratic and selfishly masculine attitude which will one day be swept away from the world by women who will not stand such treatment any longer," Shikara forecast.

"If you imagine they will become an army of Amazons, strong enough to fight men and reduce them to the position of slaves," the Marquis sneered, "they would soon find that extremely boring."

"It is better than being a slave oneself!" Shikara retorted. "When we reach the Pyramids I am sure I shall be convinced that they were built by slave labour and that the slaves were women!"

There was silence for a moment after she had finished speaking. Then the Marquis said slowly and questioningly:

"When *we* reach the Pyramids?"

Shikara flushed.

"Had you forgotten that I am not coming with you?" he asked. "Or are you scheming as to how you can get me finally to capitulate to your wishes and carry you up the Nile?"

Shikara drew in her breath.

"You know I want it above all things," she said in a low voice. "You know I shall be apprehensive if you leave me at Gibraltar or anywhere else. But I have no right to ask you to do anything you do not wish to do. You have been ... so kind ... so overwhelmingly kind already."

There was a note of sincerity in her voice and a throb of emotion behind the words which the Marquis had not heard before.

He looked at her in surprise. Then because Shikara thought she might have betrayed herself she rose from the table.

"I am sure you wish to be alone, My Lord," she said hastily.

"I certainly need time to think over what you have just said," the Marquis retorted.

"I am ... sorry," Shikara said, her eyes on his. "I did not wish to be a nuisance or importunate in any way. I gave you my promise and I will ... keep it, whatever ... happens."

Then she went from the Saloon and the door closed behind her.

"Blast it!" the Marquis ejaculated to himself. "Is any man more bedevilled by women than I am?"

At the same time, he knew it was going to be hard to put Shikara ashore as he had first intended at either Gibraltar or Algiers.

Even if he found her a ship and put her on board and saw that she had enough money for the voyage, he knew that she would arrive in Cairo without being sure that her father would be there, and having, he was sure, no other friends.

She was so young and so innocent that he told himself again that he had been wrong to introduce her to Madalena.

He had not missed the fact that Shikara had been shocked and astonished when the Portuguese woman kissed him good-night on deck.

He had had a brief but passionate affair with Madalena Monteiro in Rome two years previously.

He had been in the city with nothing to do and had met her at a party on the first night of his arrival.

They had gravitated towards each other almost instinctively, and the Marquis had known as he touched her hand that a fire leapt within them both which if encouraged could become a blaze

Because it amused him, he had deliberately gone to the theatre the following evening to sweep aside an admirer with whom she had promised to have supper and carry her off in triumph.

In the following four weeks Madalena had broken engagements and promises and seen almost nobody but himself.

It had been spring, with Rome looking particularly lovely, and their romance, if that was the right name for it, had been a physical delight that exceeded anything the Marquis had found before.

Madalena had had many lovers, and when she desired a man she gave herself as wholeheartedly to the art of love as she applied herself on the stage to the art of ballet.

It was the Marquis, well versed in the rules of never becoming satiated to the point of boredom, who finally brought their union to an end and left Rome.

He had not expected to see Madalena again, and in fact when they had put into Port Tejo he had had no intention of even enquiring if she was in the city.

It would have been easy for him to see her when she was last in Paris, but he never wished to revive the past, or to spoil what had been a charming and delightful interlude in his life by trying to resurrect dying embers.

It had been impossible to resist Madalena last night when he went ashore, although he had had no intention of making love to her unless the moment seemed right and the fire that lay between them showed itself undiminished.

It had in fact proved to be almost completely satisfactory, and yet he knew he had no desire to be embroiled again in the tempestuous, erotic atmosphere of Madalena's life.

He had done it once and it had been an enjoyable experience; but like most women of her type she was too demanding and expected a man's wholehearted attention, which included the surrendering of his mind as well as his body.

It was not in the Marquis's character to be anything but the autocrat, the leader, the commander not only of himself but of those round him.

He knew even while Madalena captivated him and aroused his desires, it was of her he had said: "Enough is as good as a feast!"

Now his thoughts were not of Madalena, but of **Shikara.**

He might have realised, he thought, that underneath that fragile appearance there was a will of iron.

She was determined, just as she had been determined to escape from her Uncle, to stay with him and if possible to inveigle him into taking her to Cairo.

"I will do nothing of the sort!" the Marquis said aloud.

But there was somehow a lack of conviction behind his assertion and he knew already that his defences were falling and he was finding it hard to abandon her to her fate.

The yacht encountered surprisingly good weather in the Mediterranean.

It was cold at night but the sun shone during the day and as they sailed eastward from Gibraltar it became warmer still, so that Shikara wore the thin gowns she had bought to wear in Egypt with only a shawl round her shoulders to protect her from the chill of the sea breezes.

The Marquis, who was on deck every daylight hour, was becoming sun-burnt and she thought it became him and that he looked if possible even more handsome than he had before.

He had not said anything about her leaving him when they reached Algiers, and yet apprehensively every day as they drew nearer to that port of call she prayed fervently that she would not be forced to go on alone.

"I love him! Oh, God, I love him!" she confessed to herself.

Yet because she was so afraid that he might guess her feelings, she forced herself to be even more argumentative and aggressive than usual and often even left him alone when she might in fact have found an excuse for staying.

Every day as they talked at mealtimes, she learnt more and more about him to make her realise how different he was from any other man she had known.

She realised of course that she could not have expected any of the young men whom she had met to be as knowledgeable and worldlywise as the Marquis. The elderly ones, like Lord Stroud, had neither the Marquis's physical attractions nor his presence and personality, which made him outstanding in any company and in any country.

He was extremely interested in her father and his work and she told him many things that her father had discovered in different lands. Then she explained why he had gone to Egypt.

"Who is this man your father was meeting?" the Marquis enquired.

"He is a Frenchman, Auguste Mariette. Papa met him when he was in the Egyptian Department in the Louvre. He and Papa had many long conversations together."

Shikara paused to say:

"He is much younger than Papa, so that in a way the friendship was rather surprising. I believe, however, that *Monsieur* Mariette is a very intelligent young man, while Papa often said that most of the men who work in Museums become as dull and fusty as the antiques they handle!"

The Marquis laughed.

"Go on with your story."

"Over a year ago *Monsieur* Mariette wrote to Papa. Papa did not know until then that he had left France, having been commissioned by the Louvre to go to Cairo to buy Coptic manuscripts.

"He said that in Egypt he saw how its ancient treasures were being plundered and he was much more interested in doing something to remedy this abuse than in haggling with antique-dealers."

"What did your father say to that?"

"Papa had said for a long time that it was absolutely disgraceful how few countries realise the value of what they possess, especially Egypt."

"I have heard that before," the Marquis remarked.

"Papa used to rage about Archaeologists, tourists,

and excavators who seem to be carried away by the passion of collecting. In fact they rob old monuments, tombs, and Temples, and make off with the treasures themselves."

"I admit it seems to be thieving on a large scale," the Marquis said.

"That is exactly what it is, and *Monsieur* Mariette explained that without some way of conserving the treasures he had found in Egypt, the future of Archaeologists in the country would be seriously jeopardised."

"What had he discovered?" the Marquis enquired.

"He told Papa he had not been in Egypt long before he noticed a most remarkable thing. Stone Sphinxes of identical appearance were displayed in private gardens by wealthy Egyptian officials, and in front of the newer Temples in Alexandria, Cairo, and Giza."

"If they were all the same they must have come from the same source."

"That is exactly what *Monsieur* Mariette thought. Then one day walking through the ruins of Saggara, a town near Cairo, he came upon a Sphinx buried all but the head in the sand near the great Step Pyramid of Zoser."

"He recognised the similarity between this Sphinx and those he had seen in Cairo and Alexandria," the Marquis remarked.

"Yes," Shikara replied, "so he dug it up and found on it an inscription recording a pronouncement relating to Apis, the Sacred Bull of Memphis. Then he knew he had found something very exciting!"

There was such a note of triumph in the way Shikara spoke that the Marquis too felt excited as he asked:

"What was that?"

"*Monsieur* Mariette realised he had found the lost Alley of the Sphinxes, which was known to have existed but up to that time had never been found."

"What happened?"

"He hired a gang of Arabs, equipped them with shovels, and set them digging. They brought one hundred forty Sphinxes to light!"

"I can realise that that was very thrilling for him," the Marquis said.

"It was then that he sat down and wrote to Papa. He was doing everything on his own and I think he felt he needed a world-famous Archaeologist and Professor to come and support him. After all, as he said in his letter, he had been sent to Cairo to buy manuscripts."

"And so your father set off?"

"He could not wait to go," Shikara replied, "especially as *Monsieur* Mariette thought he would find as well as the Alley of the Sphinxes the burial places of the Sacred Bulls."

The Marquis did not speak and after a moment Shikara said:

"I expect you know that it was not until late in Egyptian history that the likenesses of gods were given human form. Originally they were represented in animal form. There was the cow, the ram, the falcon, the ibis, the crocodile, the cat, and the serpent."

"Yes, I knew that," the Marquis answered, "and the most famous, if I am not mistaken, was the Sacred Bull of Memphis."

"That is right!" Shikara said. "The Sacred Bull was worshipped in the form of a living animal. It was housed in the Temple and attended by the Priests. Papa has often told me how when it died it was embalmed and buried with great ceremony."

"And you really think that *Monsieur* Mariette has found the burial place of the Bulls?" the Marquis asked. "There is I believe a graveyard for sacred cats, one for crocodiles, and another one for ibises, but as far as I know they have never up to now found the burial chambers of the Bulls."

"That is true," Shikara said. "Of course he may be wrong, but when Papa left he told me he was certain

that the Tombs of the Sacred Bulls would be somewhere near the Alley of the Sphinxes."

"That is something I would really like to see!" the
Marquis exclaimed.

His eyes met Shikara's and he saw the question in
them.

"All right—you win!" he said ruefully. "I admit
that you have made me curious. I will take you to
Cairo!"

Shikara gave a little cry of sheer happiness.

"Do you mean that? Do you really mean it?"

"I suppose so," the Marquis replied. "I cannot
help feeling it is showing great weakness on my part
to allow a mere woman to make me alter my plans. I
suppose you will be cock-a-hoop because you think
you have defeated me!"

"I am cock-a-hoop only because I am so grateful!"
Shikara said quickly. "I was thinking how frightened I
would be when I found myself alone and that I might
not find Papa at once when I reach Cairo. But now
that you are taking me there, it makes everything
seem wonderful . . . really wonderful!"

There was so much elation in her voice that the
Marquis felt as if he had given a child a present from
the very top of a Christmas-tree.

But when Shikara had left him and he was alone,
he found himself half-regretting the impulse that had
made him say he would take her all the way to her
destination.

'At least I shall not have her safety on my conscience,' he thought, 'and besides, I really am interested in seeing the Tombs of the Sacred Bulls.'

❋   ❋   ❋

In her cabin Shikara offered up a prayer of
thanksgiving that not only would the Marquis take
her to Cairo but also that she would not have to leave
him.

At the same time, she was not prepared to tell him how nervous she was that when they reached Cairo they would find that her father had gone elsewhere and perhaps *Monsieur* Mariette had returned to Paris.

She knew only too well how vague Archaeologists and Professors were, how time meant nothing to them, and how they seldom considered anyone else's convenience but their own.

It was quite likely, she thought, that both her father and the Frenchman had disappeared into the desert to excavate some site they had been told about.

It would never occur to either of them to let anyone know where they were going, and certainly not to inform their relatives at home of what had aroused their interest.

"Papa has always been hopelessly vague," Shikara told herself.

But never so vague that he had not communicated with her over such a long period of time.

'Perhaps,' she thought, 'one of the reasons I hate men is because of Papa's casual behaviour towards Mama and me.'

When they were all together they had been happy enough, but it was always her father's wishes that were pandered to and her mother would never think of wanting to do anything to which he did not give his permission.

When he was away or wished to travel to excavate a site in some outlandish place, he would go without a thought of how lonely her mother would be in his absence.

What was more, he never made provision of any sort for her to have the companionship of one of her relatives in his absence.

"I think Papa is very selfish!" Shikara had said once to her mother.

But in return she had only received a smile and the laughing reply of:

"What man is not? Men rule the world, Shikara,

and the sooner you realise it the better! A woman is only a secondary consideration to a man beside his work or where his interests are concerned."

The men Shikara had met had never led her to think any differently.

They had all been selfish and self-centred, and her Uncle had been the personification of everything masculine that she loathed and despised.

All his household went in fear of him; she had never known him to do a kindly action that was not to his own advantage, or even to say a kind word if it was possible to find fault.

"It is not surprising," she told herself, "that I was not prepared for anyone like the Marquis."

She had not missed the invariably pleasant way in which he spoke to his servants, nor the fact that the accommodation for the crew had been thought out with the same attention to detail as had been devoted to the cabins for himself and his guests.

'He is kind, he is generous, and he is considerate,' she thought, remembering how he had treated her.

Then the remembrance that he hated women swept over her to make her feel despairingly that he would never feel anything for her except possibly an amused tolerance.

Because she was in love, it seemed to her that time was rushing towards that inevitable moment when, having reached Cairo and seen the Tombs of the Bulls, the Marquis would inform her that he was returning to England and she would never see him again.

'Perhaps it would be better if I had never met him,' she thought sometimes in despair.

Yet because she was in love, her eyes shone more brightly and she became lovelier than she had ever before been in her life.

Hignet had placed a chair with a footrest on deck in a place protected from the wind and over which when the sun was bright there was an awning to protect her from the heat.

Sometimes to her delight when she was sitting there alone reading, the Marquis would join her, and now that she realised that he was interested in Egyptian mythology she told him many of the things which she had learnt from her father.

"I am so looking forward to seeing Alexandria," she said.

"Why particularly?" he asked.

"I think, if I am honest and because I am a woman, it is because in Alexandria there was the Palace of Cleopatra and somewhere I think there is her tomb and that of Antony."

"I had forgotten that," the Marquis said. "I was more interested in the fact that it was the city of Alexander the Great and that on the Island of Pharos there was the famous lighthouse—one of the Seven Wonders of the World."

"I like to remember that Menelaus brought his beautiful wife Helen to Egypt after the fall of Troy," Shikara replied, "and later they returned to Sparta with rich and valuable souvenirs of the visit."

"I can see that once we reach Egypt we shall have a lot to discuss" the Marquis smiled. "While you will be looking for the jewels and Palaces, I shall be thinking of the great lighthouse and the beacon light which was kept constantly burning and passed through a lens of transparent stone."

"What happened to the lighthouse?" Shikara asked. "I cannot ever remember hearing the reason why it is not there now."

"The Architect provided for the refuelling of the beacon, which could be seen as far as ninety miles out to sea, by constructing a spiral lamp up which laden horses or even wagons could ascend, carrying wood-fuel for the fire."

"And so it was burnt down," Shikara exclaimed.

"No, nothing so ordinary," the Marquis answered. "A spy in the employ of a Christian Emperor persuaded Caliph Al-Wahid that the builders had buried a great treasure under the lighthouse."

"And the temptation was too great!" Shikara cried.

"Exactly!" the Marquis agreed. "Excavations were made. The huge lantern fell and was smashed and nothing Al-Wahid or his workmen could do could put it back into place again."

"Oh, how sad!" Shikara said. "So it was destroyed by greed!"

"I am afraid so," the Marquis said, "just as greed, according to your father's friend, *Monsieur* Mariette, is depriving us of the amazing treasures that Egypt must hold hidden in the sand, the knowledge of which could benefit the whole world."

"You make me long to fight, as Papa is fighting, to preserve the past," Shikara said.

"As a mere woman," the Marquis replied provocatively, "I think really you should be concerning yourself with you own future."

Chapter Five

"I can hardly believe I am really here!" Shikara said.

"Did you doubt your own determination?" the Marquis enquired.

She smiled at him.

"Not really, because I had to reach Papa by some means or other. But I could not believe you really meant to sail up the Nile in your yacht."

She had grown more and more excited as they neared Alexandria, and as they approached Egypt the yacht had churned up for miles reddish-brown water, the mud-retained effluent of the Nile.

Then on the flat sky-line had appeared first the harbour-works, then the domed Palace of the Khedive, and then the harbour.

They had gone ashore at Alexandria to be received by beggars, hawkers, and "gully-gully" men, the conjurers who did miraculous tricks with baby chickens which made Shikara feel their lives must be very short-lived.

Shikara and the Marquis both were anxious to hasten on to Cairo, and soon they had left Alexandria behind and were steaming along the wide river with embankments rising twenty feet or so above the fields.

Everything she saw had for Shikara an enchantment: the emerald-coloured crops of maze and sugar-cane, the chocolate-coloured earth where the wooden hand-ploughs had turned it, and the dense groves of date palms and banana plantations.

She noticed in the fields that the *fellah*, or Egyptian workman, bending over his hoe, used the same kind of implement which her father had shown her in Museums labelled 3000 B.C.

Or else naked to the waist he walked behind a plough drawn by two black oxen or a camel, and the plough, Shikara knew, was exactly like those she would see later on the tomb paintings.

Despite the fact that the first railway had recently been opened between Alexandria and Cairo, the Nile still carried a lot of traffic.

The white slanting sails caught the slight wind as the boats sailed noiselessly up and down the river.

On the top of the embankments, camels passed in single file, donkeys heavily over-laden trotted in the smouldering black dust, and in the black mud of the canal banks half-naked men ceaselessly turned the handles of barrels which sucked up the waters of the Nile in the same primitive manner they had since time immemorial.

As they journeyed Shikara and the Marquis talked of Egyptian history, and she found that the Marquis was extremely interested in Napoleon's campaign in 1796.

"Do you realise," he said to Shikara, "that he sailed with a Fleet of 328 vessels, carrying 38,000 men on board—almost as large a force as Alexander commanded."

"I hate Napoleon!" Shikara cried. "He is a typical case of a man who must always be the conqueror, whatever cruelty and suffering he inflicts upon other people."

"You must admit at the same time he was a superb solidier."

"I admit nothing!" she answered. "He was supremely indifferent to how many men died in his campaigns. It was poetic justic that Nelson descended on his Fleet like an avenging angel and that a great number of French soldiers were blinded by the Egyptian eye disease!"

"You are a blood-thirsty little thing at heart!"

"I like people who build up the world, not destroy it," Shikara said crossly.

He laughed at her then, but when they went on deck after dinner to look out into the star-strewn darkness they were both of them for the moment caught up in the mystery and magic of the Egyptian night.

There was no twilight in Egypt.

There was a brief, expectant hush when it had seemed to Shikara in the vast stillness that time itself had stopped.

The first star appeared overhead, there was the shrill squeak of a bat, and the wings of darkness seemed to sweep down upon the world.

She could understand why her father had told her that the Egyptian labourers were afraid of the dark.

This sudden cessation of light falling upon the heels of golden day had inspired weird pictures of the underworld which the ancient Egyptians had painted on their tombs.

They believed that death would be like the night of Egypt, haunted by strange creatures of the imagination, half-man and half-animal.

But when the stars had come out and a faint moon had risen, there was a new light over the land, silver and mystic. The Nile became like molten silver and Shikara felt herself listening to the silence as if it would speak to her.

She was wearing one of her new gowns which she had bought in Lisbon, and she thought that when she had entered the Saloon before dinner there was a glint of admiration in the Marquis's eyes, but she could not be sure of it.

She wanted so desperately for him to admire her, but she felt she could never compete with the allurement and the seductiveness of the *Senhora*.

And yet, irresistible though the ballerina had

seemed, the Marquis had deliberately left Lisbon far sooner than there was any need, and had he not said "enough is as good as a feast"?

Shikara wondered a little wistfully how any man could have enough of a woman who was so enchanting. Then she told herself it was all part of the Marquis's dislike of women—all women—and that of course included herself.

When he came to stand beside her on deck she was pulsatingly aware of him and every nerve in her body seemed to tingle because he was beside her.

"What are you seeking?" he asked.

She glanced at him in surprise, not expecting him to be so perceptive as to realise that part of her reached out towards Egypt, feeling that spiritually it held something special for her.

Because she could not explain in words, what she felt she said:

"I think I am trying to visualise Cleopatra's great barge coming down over this very same water on her way to meet Antony. I like to think of the golden perfumed sails, the presents she had prepared for him, and the beautiful women on board, of whom of course Cleopatra herself was much the most beautiful!"

"And Antony certainly appreciated what he was offered," the Marquis said cynically.

"They fell in love with each other," Shikara said in a low voice. "He had come to conquer Egypt, but Cleopatra conquered him!"

"On the contrary," the Marquis said almost sharply, "she was the one who was conquered. She loved him and unless the books I have read are incorrect he was always her master. In fact she loved him more than he loved her!"

"They were happy," Shikara argued almost fiercely, "very happy!"

"Why not?" the Marquis answered. "She was an extremely beautiful woman!"

There was silence. Then Shikara said in a very small voice:

"Is that all that men want? For a woman to be . . . beautiful?"

The Marquis hesitated for a moment.

"If you are asking me to speak honestly," he said at last, "I think a man seeks much more, although it is something he seldom if ever finds."

"What does he seek?" Shikara asked.

The Marquis was looking out over the darkness and by the light of the stars she could see his profile quite clearly. She knew that they were talking in a manner they had never done before.

He was not being cynical or mocking, nor was he teasing her.

He was telling her what he really felt, and she held her breath for fear she should do anything to disrupt the train of his thoughts.

"I think every man, if he is truthful," the Marquis said slowly, "has an ideal in his heart of the type of woman he would wish not only to love but also to marry."

"And what would . . . she be . . . like?" Shikara asked, hardly daring to breathe the words.

"You asked me if a man wants only beauty in a woman," the Marquis replied, "but I believe that when a man loves, the woman on whom his affections are fixed always seems to be beautiful. But it is not facial appearance that is of any great consequence."

He paused for a moment before he went on:

"It is something which is deeper, something which comes from the spirit or perhaps what religious people would call the soul."

Again there was silence and as Shikara did not speak he continued:

"I cannot pretend to be a great authority like your father on ancient religions, but from what I have read, the people of the past were all seeking something greater, something beyond themselves, something which they sensed but could not actually describe in words."

His voice deepened

"That is why it is often music, painting, or sculpture which expresses what lies in a man's heart better than anything he can say in commonplace words."

"Is that . . . what you seek?" Shikara asked.

The Marquis did not answer and after a second she said:

"I think I understand, and in a way it is frightening because what is outside us is so much bigger and more powerful than we are."

She sighed.

"It makes me feel very small and . . . unimportant, and yet I want to be . . . part of it."

"No-one is really unimportant to himself," the Marquis replied, "and I believe we are extremely important in the pattern of the universe."

"How can you be sure of that?" Shikara enquired. "How can I know that I am not utterly dispensable and that if I vanished into the darkness of the night and was never seen again, it would have no effect whatever in the world? Nor would anyone care what happened to me."

The Marquis smiled at the passion behind her words and turned to look at her.

Her eyes were pools of darkness. Yet the starlight seemed to glisten on her hair, and he could see the whiteness of her neck and shoulders and the delicacy of her hands as they rested on the rail of the yacht.

"You are being very modest this evening," he said. "That is not like you."

"I am afraid," Shikara confessed, "not of physical dangers but of letting my life slip by without living, without knowing any of the things that lie beyond myself."

Her voice seemed to throb in the darkness. Then she said:

"Like you, and perhaps like everyone else, I am searching for an . . . ideal. I would be such a complete and absolute . . . failure if I did not find it."

"I think you will always find what you seek."

The Marquis sounded very reassuring and she

looked up at him, thinking how tall and broad-shouldered he seemed and that it would be impossible to be afraid of anything when he was beside her.

"You are very lovely, Shikara," he said in a low voice that was unexpectedly deep. "I would wish you to be happy."

She felt herself vibrate to the way he spoke. Then as she looked at him and he was looking down at her something magnetic seemed to pass between them.

It was something she could not explain, and yet it was there, vibrating in the air so that it was impossible for her to move, although she felt as if he drew her closer to him.

For a long moment they were both silent and still. Then slowly, as if it was inevitable, like the waters of the Nile moving beneath them, the Marquis put his arms round Shikara and drew her against him.

Just for a moment he looked down into her face, before his lips were on hers.

She could not move, she could not breathe; all that she could think was that his lips were hard and his arms seemed to encircle her completely.

Then a sensation of joy and excitement such as she had never known before seemed to rise in her throat and fled from there into her lips.

A thrill like forked lightning ran through her body so intensely that it was almost painful, and yet it was a rapture such as she had never before known or dreamt existed.

The Marquis's arms tightened and she felt that her whole being melted into his and became part of him.

She knew that this was what she had wanted since the beginning of time, and that because it was so perfect, so much a part of the Divine and came only from him, it was why she had hated all other men.

The Marquis held her closer and closer and his kiss became more intense, more demanding, until Shikara felt as if her whole being passed into his and she no longer had any identity of her own.

She was not herself but him; her lips became his lips, her body his body, and there was no division between them.

This was love!

This was the mystery and the wonder she had sought in the darkness, this was the answer to all the yearnings of her mind and the cravings of her heart.

How long the Marquis held her against him and kissed her she had no idea; she only knew that she was no longer conscious of the moving yacht, the shimmering water, the stars overhead, the darkness of the land.

There was only him in a magical golden world where she belonged to him.

At last the Marquis raised his head, and while Shikara was incapable of speech, incapable of any movement, he looked down at her and it seemed to her as if he searched her face.

Then abruptly, without speaking, he turned and walked away, leaving her alone on the deck.

❊   ❊   ❊

They arrived at Cairo the following morning and anchored to the shore.

Looking out from the port-hole of her cabin, Shikara could see that there were house-boats and Nile steamers also anchored not far away from them.

Flotillas of *giyasat*, their slim masts towering to the sky, their white sails reefed, lay together in midstream, while *celuccas* came slowly down the river laden with cargoes of sugar-cane, grain, rice, and coffee.

She had longed for this moment, longed to reach Cairo, and now she found it difficult to think of anything but the Marquis, who had kissed her last night.

She had known then that she belonged to him

and that if he left her she would never again be complete.

Never had she imagined that a kiss could be so wonderful, so perfect, and that not only her lips but every nerve in her body could be swept into an indescribable rapture.

The feeling he had evoked in her was like a flame igniting her senses, and at the same time it was part of the whole beautiful wonder of the universe.

Now she understood why everyone longed for love, why Kings gave up their thrones, nations went to war, and men died rather than lose this ecstasy which transformed them from mere human clay into gods.

"I love him . . . I love him . . . I love him . . ." Shikara whispered.

But when she had gone to bed without seeing him, she told herself that perhaps the kiss he had given her meant no more to him than the kiss he had received from the *Senhora*.

"He kissed me because it was night and because I was the only woman with him," she told herself. "If there had been another woman present he might have kissed her."

The depressing thought brought tears to her eyes but she would not let them fall.

"He hates women," she told herself, "and I am only a woman! Although I may amuse him for the moment or help him to pass the time when there is no-one else, that is all."

It made her want to scream at the frustration of it, to rush to the Marquis to fling herself on her knees at his feet and beg him to care for her.

Then she knew he would only despise her: if anything would convince him he must leave her as quickly as possible, it would be that.

She was sure that because she was what he called "a lady" he would not ask any more of her than a kiss.

With the *Senhora* it had been different. They had made love, she was sure of it. But it was something she was certain the Marquis would never suggest to her because it would be against his code of honour.

"I love him! I love him so much that I would be glad to do anything he asks of me," she told herself miserably.

But she knew he would never ask her, not, at any rate while she was under his protection and while she had no-one else but him to whom she could turn.

Even though she played with the idea that once she found her father the Marquis might suggest a different relationship, she knew it was only the foolish dream of a girl who was in love and bore no relation to fact.

'I have to face the truth that his kiss was just an impulse of the moment,' Shikara thought. 'He has never so much as held my hand before, but perhaps it was the darkness and the magnetism of Egypt, or just because I had said I was lonely and afraid.'

Whatever the reason, after he had kissed her he had gone away. Perhaps although to her it had been magical and wonderful beyond words, to him it had meant nothing!

It was still very early in the morning, but Shikara dressed and went up on deck to look at the ships on the river and the people moving along the road which bordered their anchorage.

She could see the Mosques and minarets rising high above the roofs of the buildings on the other side of the water, and she knew that the most spectacular was the Mosque of Mohammed Ali, perched high on the rock of the Citadel.

Its slender Turkish minarets rose above everything else in Cairo and Shikara wondered if it would be possible for her to visit the Mosque.

She heard a step and thought it might be the Marquis, but it was a steward.

"Good-morning, Miss!" he said respectfully. "I've taken your breakfast to your room."

"Thank you," Shikara said.

She went below, not liking to ask if the Marquis had already breakfasted.

When she had finished the coffee and fresh rolls she wondered whether she should go in search of the Marquis, or find Hignet and ask what were the plans for the day. Then almost as if she had called him Hignet came to the door of her cabin.

"His Lordship's compliments, Miss, and if you are ready to go ashore he's waiting for you."

"I would like that very much," Shikara replied.

Springing up, she quickly took a broad-brimmed hat that she had bought in Lisbon from the cupboard and having put it on her head collected the white sunshade that she had bought according to the Marquis's instructions.

"It's always better in the heat to get off very early," Hignet said. "I think His Lordship intends to take you out to the Pyramids."

"That is where I want to go," Shikara said almost breathlessly, and picking up the white hand-bag which matched her gown she ran from the cabin up onto the deck.

The Marquis was waiting for her and she felt her heart turn somersaults in her breast. On the other side of the gangway was an open carriage drawn by two horses.

"I thought we should waste no time," he said as Shikara appeared, "but go at once in search of *Monsieur* Mariette, and ask him what has happened to your father."

"That is what I am anxious to do," Shikara answered.

She tried to read the expression on the Marquis's face, but it seemed to her that he was deliberately not looking at her.

There was something reserved about him, as if he had withdrawn and the barriers that had existed between them before had been set up again.

She stepped into the carriage and tried to think

how excited she was at the hope of finding her father after all these months of silence.

But instead she was vividly conscious of the Marquis, realising how smart he looked in a white suit, and at the same time afraid that he was regretting what had happened the night before.

They drove through streets crowded with the traffic of donkeys, carts, carriages, camels, and oxen.

From the shops came the scents of musk, attar of roses, incense, and coffee. Soon they were clear of the city and its veiled women and were driving out on a raised road which Shikara knew led towards the Pyramids.

"I have been making enquiries," the Marquis said after they had travelled for some way in silence, "and I understand that *Monsieur* Mariette is in fact to be found on the site he is investigating."

"So he is here?" Shikara asked. "I was half-afraid he might have returned to France."

"The idea had crossed my mind," the Marquis said, "which would account for his not answering your letter."

"Perhaps Papa is with him," Shikara suggested hopefully.

The Marquis did not answer and she had the feeling that he thought it unlikely.

The horses that were drawing them travelled quickly and soon they were in sight of the Pyramids, standing out against the desert of sand.

Although Shikara longed to stop and visit them, she knew that the Marquis was right and that the first thing they must do on their arrival in Egypt was to seek her father.

Although she tried to keep the thought from her mind, one question repeated and repeated itself as they drove along:

'If my father is here, how long will the Marquis stay once he has given me into his care?'

Because she was shy she only glanced at him

sideways out of the corner of her eyes and as he did not seem inclined to speak she too was silent.

They drove past the first Pyramids and now the Great Step Pyramid of Zoser came into sight and the palm trees which surrounded the building which the Marquis told Shikara was the Temple of Ptah.

There were stones and great slabs of marble and rock everywhere.

As they stepped from the carriage Shikara thought for a moment that it would be impossible to re-create anything out of such a confusion of rocks and sand.

The Marquis was walking ahead of her, when she saw a little to their left the Avenue of Sphinxes.

There was no mistaking that this was where Mariette had made his wonderful discovery two years earlier, and she stood entranced.

The Avenue followed a relatively straight course for about six hundred yards, then turned sharply to the left, leading to the front of a small Temple before which was ranged a remarkable semi-circle of statues.

They walked towards it, and seeing some workmen the Marquis asked for *Monsieur* Mariette.

They pointed the way and Shikara and the Marquis descending a steep shaft into the ground heard voices and the sound of digging at the end of a long chamber.

"Is *Monsieur* Mariette there?" the Marquis asked. His voice seemed to echo back at them, and for the moment there was no answer.

Then slowly coming down what Shikara learnt later was the long burial chamber of the Sacred Bulls, they saw a man.

"Are you looking for me, *Monsieur?*" he enquired in French.

"You are *Monsieur* Auguste Mariette?" the Marquis enquired.

"*Oui, Monsieur.*"

"I am the Marquis of Linwood, and I have

brought you Professor Richard Bartlett's daughter, who has come to Egypt in search of her father."

Monsieur Mariette gave a cry of astonishment, then turning towards Shikara he held out both his hands.

"*Mademoiselle*," he exclaimed. "Your father spoke about you so often that I feel already I know you."

Shikara curtseyed and was a little surprised when he raised both her hands to his lips, one after another.

"I am honoured—deeply honoured—that you should have come here," Monsieur Mariette said, "and I only wish I had better news to tell you about your father."

"He is . . . dead?" Shikara asked in a low voice.

Monsieur Mariette made a little gesture with his hand.

"The truth is, *Mademoiselle*, that I do not know."

"Then where is he? What could have happened to him?" Shikara asked.

"I must explain," *Monsieur* Mariette answered.

His shirt-sleeves were turned up and he wore no tie, but nevertheless even with his clothes covered in sand there was a dignity and an air of authority about him which Shikara felt commanded respect.

"Shall we sit down, *Mademoiselle?*" he suggested, and looked round him vaguely.

There was some fallen masonry and because he seemed to expect it of her Shikara seated herself, although the Marquis remained standing.

Monsieur Mariette sat down opposite her.

"What . . . happened?" she asked as if she was impatient to come to the point.

"Your father, as you know, joined me over a year ago," *Monsieur* Mariette began. "It was when I first discovered the Sphinxes and I had the idea that the Tomb of the Sacred Bulls could not be far away."

"That is what you said in your letter to Papa."

"I was right," *Monsieur* Mariette said, "and in fact I can now show you the catacomb for the Apis burials, and not only the vaults but a tomb of burials made in the reign of Ramses II intact and unviolated by robbers."

"How wonderful!" Shikara exclaimed. "And was Papa here when you found them?"

"Yes, indeed," *Monsieur* Mariette replied. "That was on March nineteenth last year, and your father started to catalogue the contents of the sarcophagi."

"What did they contain?" Shikara asked.

"A collection of bones and other animal material in a poor state of preservation," *Monsieur* Mariette replied, "but there was also a quantity of funereal statuettes, gold ornaments, and some other objects of inestimable value."

"If that was last March," Shikara said, "why did Papa not write to me as he always used to do?"

"I am sure he intended to, *Mademoiselle*," *Monsieur* Mariette replied, "but your father was as excited as I was at finding the catacombs of the Sacred Bulls and I am afraid we found it impossible to think of anything else."

Shikara did not speak and he added apologetically:

"There was an enormous amount of excavation to do which involved tremendous problems. . . ."

He made a gesture with his hands as he spoke and went on:

"You can see the sand and dust that lies thick everywhere. It creates a kind of fog, fine and all-penetrating. There were falls of rock and sometimes the candles we used could not be kept alight without difficulty."

"I can understand that Papa would forget about me," Shikara said, "but what has happened to him?"

Monsieur Mariette drew in his breath.

"Again I must give you the truthful answer, *Mademoiselle*: I do not know!"

"You do not know?" Shikara repeated.

"He disappeared!"

"How could he have done that?"

"He was staying near here where the accommodation is fairly uncomfortable and the houses are so small that we were not together."

"Go on!" Shikara urged.

"One morning your father did not turn up as I had expected and I thought perhaps he was occupied with some of the writing he had to do. I meant to call on him that evening, but I was tired and left it until the following day.

"When he did not appear then, I sent someone to find him, and the reply came back that the people in the house where he was lodging thought he was me.

"I was not perturbed. As you know, your father was very vague and sometimes went into Cairo if there was some information he required or if he needed special tools with which to clean the objects we found."

"You must have thought it strange when he was away for so long," Shikara said.

"It only gradually dawned on me that there was anything peculiar about his nonappearance," *Monsieur* Mariette admitted. "Although we were very close in our work we both liked to go our own ways and never interfered with each other."

"That sounds very like Papa."

"Then at last I really became worried," *Monsieur* Mariette continued, "and I found that in fact your father had completely vanished!"

"How could he have done that?"

"I do not know," he answered. "I went to his lodgings and found everything just as he had left it. There was a half-written letter to you, but otherwise there was nothing of importance except the objects we had discovered in the sarcophagi."

"What steps did you take to find him?" the Marquis asked.

He had said nothing until now, and both Shikara and *Monsieur* Mariette started when he interrupted their conversation.

"I asked everyone locally if they had seen him," the Frenchman replied, "and they were all convinced that he had gone off on a trip into the desert to look at some other site.

"We had in fact talked of looking for tombs at Abydos, but I could not really believe that the Professor would go there without me or at least informing me of his intention."

"So what did you do?" the Marquis persisted.

Monsieur Mariette looked embarrassed.

"Quite frankly, My Lord," he said after a moment, "I did not know what to do. I knew that the Professor would not like too many enquiries made about him. I had asked nobody's permission in inviting him to join me, and the French Government, which has allowed me to continue my work and given me a substantial grant of money, is very jealous of other nations having any part in the discoveries which I have made."

"I can understand that," the Marquis said. "But at the same time, the Professor is a man of distinction and his disappearance cannot remain a secret forever."

"I am aware of that," *Monsieur* Mariette answered, "and I intend to employ a detective, or at least some responsible person, to make a thorough search for him."

As he spoke, Shikara, and she thought the Marquis would think the same, realised that *Monsieur* Mariette, intent on his excavations, had just let things drift.

He might have been perturbed and worried by her father's disappearance, but nothing could wean him away from the excitement and thrill of his discoveries.

"You must accept my deepest regret about what has happened, *Mademoiselle*," he said to Shikara, "and I assure you that my respect and admiration for your father increased a thousand-fold by the tremendous assistance he gave me while we were working together."

"Thank you," Shikara replied.

"I suggest, *Monsieur*," the Marquis said, "that you

come with us now to a place where we can have luncheon. As you will appreciate, this has been a shock to Miss Bartlett, and there are a great many details she would like clarified. I think we can do so in more comfortable circumstances than down here in the dust and dark."

"Of course, My Lord. I shall be very pleased to do anything you ask," *Monsieur* Mariette replied.

But Shikara could not help feeling that he was regretting the hours he must spend away from his excavations.

Because she thought it would please him, she asked if she could see what he had already discovered; and there was a light in his eyes and a lilt to his voice as he took her along the corridor which extended for many chambers, containing the mummified remains of the Bulls.

There was an eeriness, Shikara thought, which came perhaps from any place associated with death and burial. But she was deeply interested and there was no doubt that the Marquis was entranced by what he saw.

Shikara too was extremely impressed by the questions he asked and the knowledge he appeared to have about the Sacred Bulls.

Proceeding from one burial chamber to another, Mariette showed them the sarcophagi in which the Bulls had been buried.

They were made of black and red granite, each one having been quarried in one piece, weighing about seventy-two tons and measuring nine feet in height.

"Had a great deal of plundering been done?" the Marquis enquired as they climbed away from the darkness towards the sunlight.

"I have found two tombs intact," *Monsieur* Mariette replied, "but of course the plunderers had done inestimable damage, not only by stealing the funereal statuettes but also by knocking down walls and rendering the roofs unsafe in many places."

"Were they modern plunderers or ancient ones?"
the Marquis enquired.

Monsieur Mariette shrugged his shoulders.

"Plunderers have existed all through the ages," he
answered, "and I find myself hating them more every
time I realise what records of history they have destroyed and how much knowledge has been lost."

"I can understand that," the Marquis agreed.

When they reached the carriage, *Monsieur* Mariette kept them waiting while he repaired to a small
tent standing near his excavations and in which apparently he kept a change of clothing.

He came to them after a short delay, looking very
much more presentable, and Shikara realised that he
was in fact an attractive young man.

She reckoned from what her father had told her
that he was only thirty-one, and it was amazing how
much he had achieved in the teeth of opposition from
the authorities and especially the agents of the Khedive, the Ruler of Egypt, who had tried at one time to
shut down the dig and confiscate what had been
found.

"Of course," *Monsieur* Mariette said with engag-
ing frankness as he related what had happened, "I
have been digging here without the appropriate permission, and had expected such intervention for some
time."

"But you are now legally entitled to excavate?"
the Marquis asked.

"Thankfully, yes," *Monsieur* Mariette replied,
"but I always run the risk of unwelcome visitors and
the dealers in Cairo, who have an easy sale for burial
bronzes and of course for anything that is gold."

Looking at some of his workmen, he added in a
worried voice:

"I can trust no-one! The men who are digging for
me try to conceal any small objects they unearth,
knowing they have a ready and ever-widening market
for them"

"That must make things very difficult for you," Shikara sympathised.

"Your father thought we had worse petty pilfering in Egypt than anywhere else in the world," *Monsieur* Mariette informed her.

They managed to obtain a rather unappetising meal at a small guest-house near the Pyramids.

Shikara was not interested in what she ate, but she thought the Marquis looked somewhat disdainfully at the food which he was served, while *Monsieur* Mariette ate everything that was put in front of him.

Now that they were away from the catacombs, he became less of an Archaeologist and more of an ardent young Frenchman.

Shikara realised that he found her attractive and there was that look in his eyes which she had seen before and had always disliked.

But because she admired *Monsieur* Mariette and because he had been a friend of her father she found herself enjoying his company and even the compliments he paid her.

"Your father spoke of you so often, *Mademoiselle*," he said. "He told me how beautiful you were, and now I see that he was not exaggerating!"

Shikara smiled.

"I cannot believe that you and Papa talked about anything but your discoveries."

"Sometimes in the evenings we would become very sentimental about the people we had left behind," *Monsieur* Mariette said.

"Papa was used to being on his own, but you, after living in Paris, *Monsieur,* must find it very strange."

"I love the desert, I love it passionately!" *Monsieur* Mariette replied. "But sometimes, *Mademoiselle,* I long for a woman like yourself to be with me— someone who would understand what I was doing, to encourage and inspire me."

The Marquis pushed back his chair, which made a scraping noise along the wooden floor.

"I think we should discuss the main object of our visit, Shikara," he said abruptly, "and that is to discover what steps have been taken to find your father."

"What can we do?" Shikara asked *Monsieur* Mariette.

"I honestly do not know," he replied. "You can go to the authorities but they will not be very interested, and, as I have said, they may be annoyed because your father was an Englishman and as such not responsible to the French Government for anything that is discovered here."

"Papa would not want to take away anything from Egypt," Shikara said.

"You know that and I know that, *Mademoiselle,*" *Monsieur* Mariette replied, "but it would be very difficult to convince anyone in authority that it was the truth."

"It certainly appears to make our task very difficult," the Marquis said dryly.

He called for the bill, then said:

"I suggest, *Monsieur,* that as it is getting towards the hottest part of the day Miss Bartlett and I should return to Cairo. Perhaps we could call on you again tomorrow, and if you have any other thoughts as to what can be done we shall be interested to hear them."

Monsieur Mariette bowed.

"I am sure Miss Bartlett would also like her father's belongings to be packed up and given into her keeping," the Marquis added.

"There is not very much, I think," *Monsieur* Mariette said vaguely. "And I left them where he was lodging."

"In which case they may have also disappeared," the Marquis remarked.

Shikara looked at him in perplexity.

She had the feeling that the Marquis was deliberately making it uncomfortable for *Monsieur* Mariette, but there was nothing she could say except to thank the Frenchman very warmly for all he had shown them.

"It has been a very great pleasure," *Monsieur* Mariette said. There was no doubt from the tone of his voice that he spoke with all sincerity.

"I want to see you tomorrow," he added in a low voice. "I am sure by that time I shall have thought of something that may be of help."

He held her hand in his, then as he had done before raised it to his lips, although Shikara knew it was unconventional to kiss the hand of an unmarried girl.

Then he left them and hurried away in a manner which made her sure he was anxious to get back to his excavations.

"I am very sorry about your father," the Marquis said as they drove back to Cairo.

"I suppose it is not worse than I expected," Shikara answered. "I really had very little hope that he was alive."

"You are now convinced that he is dead?" the Marquis asked.

"I feel there can be no other explanation. But how did he die? And why? And where? That is what I would like to know."

She sighed, then went on:

"I knew as soon as I saw the vaults that Papa would never have left so suddenly when there was so much left to excavate, so much more to discover. It was just the sort of place he adored, and he would have worked until the last possible stone was uncovered and catalogued."

"I am sorry," the Marquis said quietly.

Shikara did not reply.

A cloud of depression seemed to encompass her.

She was thinking not so much of her father's death but the fact that now that he had gone she was alone, completely alone in the world.

The future seemed very dark and empty.

Chapter Six

As it had grown very hot Shikara rested after luncheon, but she knew that the Marquis had gone ashore and she wondered where he had gone.

She had not been alone with him except in the open carriage since they had left the excavations and *Monsieur* Mariette.

She had a feeling that he was in a strange mood, which she did not understand, and it upset her because she was certain that it was somehow connected with the fact that he had kissed her last night.

She could not imagine why that should trouble him.

She herself had only to think of it to recapture that wonder and rapture she had felt when his lips held hers and she seemed to melt into him and they became no longer two people but one.

"That is what I felt," Shikara told herself, "but obviously it was very different for him—just a moment's interest in me due to the magic of the night, and now he has gone back to hating me again."

She felt as if she could hardly bear to contemplate his hatred of her as a woman, while in other ways he had been everything that was kindness and consideration.

"Perhaps," she told herself dismally, "he has gone to arrange for my journey back to England."

She was sure he would never allow her to stay

alone in Egypt, and now that she had seen both Cairo
and Alexandria she knew her original idea of staying
and finding work here was quite impossible.

The place was too big, too foreign, too alien in
every way to the life she had lived at home.

She had travelled, but that was with her father
and mother and was very different from being a
young girl unchaperoned in an alien city.

She thought perhaps she might ask *Monsieur*
Mariette if she could work with him, but she knew
how much the Archaeologists she had known in the
past had fought against the intrusion of women on
any site in which they were interested.

Shikara had thought that they resented it even
when her mother and she were shown round the
places her father was investigating.

She was therefore quite certain that although
Monsieur Mariette had looked at her with admiration,
he would want to confine their acquaintance to the
times when he was not actively employed in excavations.

Although he had taken Shikara and the Marquis
through the burial chambers, he had moved quickly
and Shikara felt she had not had a chance by the flickering candlelight to see the sarcophagi clearly or to
get a real impression of what she knew was a long-lost
cult.

Always when she had been to excavations with
her father in the past he had said to her:

"Do not just look, but think and feel. Let your
perception visualise what these people were like all
those centuries ago. Try to get in touch with their vibrations. It will teach you more than a thousand
books."

Shikara had tried to follow his instructions but
there had been no chance of doing anything but listening when *Monsieur* Mariette was pointing out the
places that had been plundered and the work he and
her father had completed.

There had also been the Arab workmen tapping

away at the unexposed tombs and carrying away the
baskets filled with sand along the long burial chamber.

There had been an unending file of them passing
all the time, and Shikara found herself continually
moving out of their way and being aware of their dark
eyes staring at her with curiosity.

"I must have looked very strange to them in my
white gown,' she thought to herself.

But she realised that they intruded on her
thoughts and her feelings, and she felt a sudden longing to use the perception that her father had taught
her.

Perhaps, who knows, she might have some idea of
what had happened to him, if she could be alone in
the quietness of the tomb.

She did not sleep during her rest, but lay plan-
ning what she would say to the Marquis. When she
heard him come on board she rose and went to find
him.

He was not in the Saloon as she had hoped, but
was standing up on deck looking across the Nile.

It was a very colourful picture and the great river
seemed to be a hive of activity.

There were also boats continually coming to the
side of the yacht, offering to sell fruit, necklaces, rugs,
and every other kind of merchandise.

The Marquis tried to ignore them, but the Egyptian salesmen were very persistent and refused to go
away.

It was therefore impossible for Shikara to speak
to him privately in such circumstances.

So they discussed the scene and the Marquis
pointed out some of the buildings of interest on the
opposite bank until it was time to change for dinner.

Shikara went below and after a cool bath which
Hignet had prepared for her she put on one of her
pretty new gowns and looked in the mirror, hoping
the Marquis would think her attractive.

"Last night he kissed me," she told herself, and felt a thrill run through her at the memory.

Could anything have been more wonderful or more perfect?

And yet he had apparently forgotten it, or now in the daylight she no longer had any attraction for him.

She longed when they were on deck to ask him why he had gone into the town, but she had been too shy and at the same time afraid.

Suppose he had arranged for her to return to England?

There seemed no doubt now that her father was dead and that her Uncle was now her undisputed Guardian.

She thought of Lord Stroud waiting for her, and she knew that once she returned she would no longer be able to escape him but would have to obey her Uncle's wishes.

"I would rather die!" she said as she said before, but this time she meant it.

She might be afraid to be alone in Egypt; but that was nothing compared to the fear she would experience if she had to marry a man who repulsed her, a man who would legally be entitled to touch and embrace her.

She knew that she would shrink in horror and disgust from any man other than the Marquis.

"Death is not the most terrifying thing in the world," she told herself.

Yet there had been something eerie in the darkness of the burial chamber which had made her long to live.

She thought that not only in the Egyptian mind but in everyone else's death was the dark and life was the sunshine. As far as she was concerned, being in the sunshine meant being with the Marquis.

Without him there was only darkness and a loneliness that she could hardly bear to contemplate.

Then with a pride that had always been very

much a part of her character Shikara told herself that if the Marquis did not want her she must leave him, as she had promised, without making a scene.

She knew that he would be contemptuous and despise her if she broke her word.

She thought she could bear anything rather than that he should leave her in disgust because she had become an intolerable nuisance.

She went up to the Saloon for dinner with her head held high, conscious that if she could not measure up to the allurements of the *Senhora,* at least she looked her best.

Now that the heat of the day was abating, there was a breeze blowing down the river and it made the whole yacht seem cool and pleasant.

There was the soft lap of the water against the sides and from the shore came the scent of the flowering shrubs which grew wild along the river bank.

It had an enchantment which Shikara would have enjoyed if her thoughts could have been centred on anything except the Marquis.

He had changed for dinner and she thought that no man could look more magnificent or more attractive as he rose to his feet when she entered the Saloon.

"You are rested?" he asked.

She smiled at him and he went on without waiting for her reply:

"I realise what you learnt today has been a shock for you. It was also very hot and I thought it would be pleasant if we had dinner tonight on deck."

"I would like that," Shikara said.

She found that the stewards had erected an awning and the place where they were to dine was screened on one side from the curious gaze of the passers-by.

The table was decorated with flowers and there was a long cool drink which tasted of limes, which Shikara found delicious.

After the very indifferent luncheon they had

eaten, the Chef's dishes would have enticed a far more fastidious appetite than hers.

The Marquis talked of Egyptian history while they were being served, and only when Shikara had finished a cup of sweet Turkish coffee did she look across the table at him to say:

"I have . . . something to . . . ask you."

"What is it?" he enquired.

She had a feeling he was slightly apprehensive.

She was aware that while he talked most interestingly during dinner there had been something impersonal about every subject on which they had touched.

It was as if he was deliberately avoiding anything that could possibly become intimate or be construed as anything but casual conversation between two people who were little more than acquaintances.

Shikara had only to look at the Marquis to feel her whole being reaching out to him.

But because she felt he did not want her, she tried desperately hard with what was an admirable self-control to behave as he appeared to wish her to do.

Yet all the time she knew that her whole being ached for him and she wanted beyond her hope of Heaven to feel his lips on hers again.

Now when they were alone she knew it was her opportunity to tell him what she wanted and after a moment's pause she said tentatively:

"You will think it very . . . strange of me, but I feel I must go back to *Monsieur* Mariette's excavations at Memphis."

"Tonight?" the Marquis enquired.

"Yes, tonight when the workmen will have gone and *Monsieur* Mariette will have left for the day."

"Why do you want to do that?" the Marquis enquired.

Shikara hesitated a moment, then she said:

"I want to get the real . . . feeling of the place. I have an idea, it may be quite . . . absurd, that it will make me feel ... closer to Papa, that I might even be ... aware of what ... happened to him."

"Do you mean that you will know clairvoyantly?" the Marquis asked.

"I suppose you might call it that," Shikara answered. "It is what Papa called 'using one's sixth sense.' It was what he always used himself when he wanted to know if an excavation was worth undertaking. He was always right even though there was nothing to see except rocks and sand."

"And you wish to go on this expedition alone?" the Marquis asked.

Shikara did not speak but she looked at him, her eyes very wide and pleading in her small face.

There was no need to put into words what she asked; she felt almost as if she said aloud how much she wanted him with her—how much she always wanted him.

He was separated from her by the table, decorated with flowers, yet they spoke to each other without words and for a moment their spirits met and there was an understanding which seem to have existed between them all through eternity.

Then the Marquis answered:

"Very well, if that is what you want I will take you."

He saw the light come into Shikara's eyes. Then she looked away from him as if she was shy and said quietly:

"Thank you ... very much!"

She went below to get a shawl to put over her shoulders in case it should grow cooler later on and she picked up a chiffon scarf for her hair.

She thought that the dust moving all the time in the darkness of the burial chamber would settle on her head and she disliked the thought of it.

When she came up on deck it was to find that the Marquis was waiting for her and on the shore there was an open carriage like they had used once already that day.

It was still daylight but Shikara knew it would not be long before the sun would sink with its usual swiftness and the stars and moon would shine over the Pyramids.

She had longed to see them at night with the Marquis at her side, but now she was uncertain of what he was thinking and she was depressingly sure that he would not, this evening, be moved romantically by the beauty of the scenery or by her.

It seemed to her that he sat deliberately a little further away from her in the carriage than necessary.

They travelled at a quick pace and Shikara felt she had nothing to say except what lay hidden secretly in her heart.

Soon they were free of the houses of Cairo and out in the desert, and now there was the strange exquisite beauty of the Pyramids, golden in the setting sun, their pointed tops silhouetted against the translucence of the sky.

"Of the Seven Wonders of the Ancient World," the Marquis remarked, "the Pyramids alone still survive the ravages of time and the destructive hand of man."

He spoke coldly and impersonally, but Shikara longed to put her hand into his and to ask if the Pyramids were to him as mysterious and exciting as they were to her.

Always she had thought in the past that when one saw anything very beautiful or very exciting it was something that must be shared.

She had understood what her father felt when at every new development in his explorations he would want to find another Archaeologist with whom he could share his discovery, or failing such a man would often be prepared to display his finds to her mother or herself.

It was as if any soul-disturbing experience one could not be selfish enough to keep to oneself, and Shikara felt now as if the sheer enchantment of the Pyramids was something she wanted to give to the Marquis, as if it was a present.

She could not however express what she was feeling and they drove on. As darkness fell they came to the Great Step Pyramid of Zoser and their driver drew his horses to a standstill.

They were not at the place where they had stopped earlier in the day, but in the half-light with the stars just beginning to twinkle in the sky it was easy to see that by walking a little way they would come to the Avenue of the Sphinxes.

It was easier to walk than to try to explain to the driver that he must turn his horses round, and Shikara and the Marquis stepped out of the carriage.

The Marquis told the man to wait by some palm trees and putting his hand under Shikara's elbow he helped her over the sand and stones towards the Avenue of Sphinxes.

Shikara felt as they walked side by side between the rows of statues, half-man and half-beast, as if she and the Marquis were a Priest and Priestess moving towards the Temple.

The Marquis had brought with him a candle-lantern, which Hignet had put into the carriage for them together with a box of matches before they left.

"This is the very best lantern we have on board, M'Lord," he had said to the Marquis, "and it's a better type than anything those Gyppies use."

"Thank you," the Marquis had said. "I am sure it will prove adequate."

Shikara thought now that she might have forgotten a candle if she had come alone, and she knew too that he carried in his coat a small pistol.

She had seen him slip it out of sight as she came on deck, and while she had not commented on it, she knew it was a wise precaution.

It had made her aware that the Marquis thought the project she was undertaking might prove to be a dangerous one.

She could not believe it possible that there would be any danger in visiting the Tombs of the Apis Bulls, but she supposed there might be a chance of visitors

either to the Pyramids or to any other part of the desert being set upon by thieves.

It made her realise that it was in fact a foolish
idea that she should ever go to such places alone.

She had seen the beggars swarming in Cairo and
in Alexandria, and she had realised that without the
protection of a man her hand-bag and any jewellery
she wore would have soon disappeared.

They reached the entrance of what looked like a
kind of Temple comparable with those built in honour
of the Egyptian nobility.

The Marquis stopped to light the candle in the
lantern and now it was easy to see the steep shaft
which led down to the long burial chamber.

He went ahead and Shikara took his hand as he
assisted her down the shaft into the warm dusty
darkness.

Now, as she had expected, there was the strange
deep silence of the dead and the smell of the past,
which seemed, she thought, always to exist in burial
grounds.

She moved ahead of the Marquis as the flickering
candle made the separate chambers where the Bulls
had been buried seem like dark caverns.

The plunderers had pushed the heavy covers off
the sarcophagi.

Some had been smashed so that they lay broken
on the ground, and some, after being despoiled, had
already been buried again by the eternally shifting
sand.

Shikara moved on down the passage-way, aware
that the airlessness made it hard to breathe, and yet
determined to reach the end where the unrifled tombs
were still being excavated.

The lantern threw a circle of light round her and
to the Marquis she was a waif moving silently ahead
of him, the scarf with which she had covered her hair
gleaming white in the darkness.

Shikara stopped.

She had almost reached the end of the passage

and she wanted to think, to concentrate like a medium in a trance, so that she could immerse herself in the past.

Then unexpectedly and sharply there was the sound of voices!

She turned and found that the Marquis was just behind her and that he too had turned his head to listen.

Men were speaking to one another in Arabic and Shikara realised the newcomers were descending the shaft behind them into the burial chamber.

The Marquis lifted the candle-lantern and blew it out. Then as Shikara waited in surprise he put out his hand and pulled her from the passage-way into one of the burial places at the side of it.

She felt the surface of a granite sarcophagus and there was just room between it and the wall for them to stand, Shikara on the inside and the Marquis nearest to the passage.

The sound of men talking came nearer, their voices deliberately lowered, so that Shikara could not hear what they were saying.

Then there was the faint light of a candle and Shikara realised that quite a number of men had entered the burial chamber.

She moved a little further round the sarcophagus and now she saw that the wall on the other side, which divided it from the tomb of another Bull, had been demolished.

She could see across the broken sarcophagus beside them into the passage-way.

The light came nearer and suddenly she could see the turbanned heads of a number of men.

She counted—there were six of them.

They were advancing, but suddenly they stopped and she heard a clanking sound as if they threw some tools down to the sandly floor.

"Better light more candles," one of them said in Arabic.

"We shall need them," another man replied in a deeper voice. "The unopened tomb is at the far end."

With a start Shikara realised who they were.

They were plunderers who had come to open the tomb which *Monsieur* Mariette had told them about, the Tomb of the Bull that had been buried in the reign of Ramses II.

One he had already excavated, but the other was so far intact.

Shikara felt a surge of anger that these plunderers should steal the contents of the tomb so that they would be lost forever.

She thought of confronting them and telling them what she thought of their thieving ways. Then, even as the idea came into her mind, she heard one of the men say:

"Someone had better be on guard."

"I'll guard you," another man replied. "Did I not guard you when the Englishman interfered? Roaring like a lion, he would have carried you all to prison if I had not silenced him!"

Other candles must have been lit; for now Shikara could see the men more clearly and the man who was talking was young, with a white turban on his head.

Another man, who was older and whose face was lined, said:

"Hush, Ali, do not boast. If anyone should hear, you'd be executed for murder!"

"I'm not afraid," Ali retorted boastfully. "Trust me as you have trusted me before. My knife has served you well, and it will serve you again if we are interrupted."

"Very well, then," the older man said almost grudgingly, "you be on guard. The rest of us had better get to work."

Shikara was suddenly conscious that the Marquis was very close to her. She knew that he had drawn his pistol from his pocket and that he was tense.

The meaning of what the men had been saying swept over her with a feeling of unutterable horror.

These were the men who had killed her father!

What was more, these robbers and murderers would undoubtedly kill the Marquis and her if they were discovered.

She felt herself begin to tremble as she realised that there were six of them—five to do the excavating, and the one called Ali to keep guard.

She thought frantically that with a pistol which held only two bullets it would be impossible for the Marquis to protect them both from men who would kill without hesitation rather than be discovered.

She heard another man, who had not previously spoken, say:

"Would not it be best to look and see if there is anyone about before we start working? Remember, the Englishman took us by surprise."

"If there was anyone here we should have seen a light," replied the older man who had spoken before.

"I'll look for you," Ali said. "You start digging. It'll take time and the night does not last forever."

"Who's giving orders?" another asked.

"Ali's talking sense," someone else said. "There are lots of hiding places here and we don't want to be taken by surprise."

"No, indeed," someone agreed. "You remember what happened last week at Abydos."

"That was a near squeak," a man groaned.

Shikara felt the Marquis's left arm go round her to hold her against him. She realised that he held his pistol in his right hand and that he was holding her close because he sensed that she was afraid.

She was trembling because the whole scene was so strange and terrifying—the flickering lights of the candles, the men's heads she could just see above the broken wall, and their revealing conversation, which only she could understand because the Marquis did not speak Arabic.

At the same time, she thought, he must be aware

that they were in a dangerous position and he would know she was frightened because he could feel her trembling against him.

The Marquis was in fact very much aware of their danger and although he could not speak Arabic he knew well how ruthless the plunderers of the tombs could be if they were discovered.

All through the ages there had been fights and murders committed by one gang of thieves when they encountered another.

Every Archaeologist told stories of how he had been obliged to fight off robbers who sometimes attacked a site even in broad daylight.

He was surprised that Mariette had not placed a guard at his excavation site and he supposed that it was because the sarcophagus of a Bull was not so valuable from the thieves' point of view as the Tomb of a Pharaoh.

When they visited the place in the morning, he had understood that on certain days of the year or on the occasion of the death or funeral rites of an Apis, the inhabitants of Memphis came to pay a visit to the god in his burial place.

In memory of this act of piety they left a *stele,* or square-shaped upright stone, rounded at the top, which was let into the walls of the tomb.

It had previously been inscribed with words of homage to the god and the name of the visitor and his family.

Those, the Marquis knew, were of the greatest historical importance, although of no cash value to any thief.

If these were broken or defaced by vandals or roughly handled by excavators, the history of Egypt would be very much the poorer.

It was therefore remiss of Mariette not to have taken more care—but how, the Marquis wondered, could he have anticipated that the thieves would come to the very last tomb and in such numbers?

He was wondering if a shot fired suddenly into

the ceiling would scare them, or whether it would be better to kill one of their number and just pray that the rest would run away.

He knew, without understanding a word of what was being said, that they would not hesitate if it suited them to kill both himself and Shikara and bury their bodies in the sand where they were unlikely ever to be found.

That, he had already surmised, was what had happened to Professor Bartlett, and he cursed himself for a fool for letting Shikara persuade him into coming here tonight without bringing with him several of the crew to protect them.

If only they had stopped at the proper entrance, where they had gone in this morning, the thieves would have seen their carriage and doubtless postponed their robbery to another night.

But as it was, their horses waiting near the palm trees must have gone unobserved.

The Marquis's fingers tightened on his pistol.

Already he could see that the men were picking up their tools from the floor, and one of their number was shining a light on the first sarcophagus at the entrance to the burial chamber.

Soon they would reach where he and Shikara were standing. It would be impossible for them to hide from the candlelight and they would be revealed.

Now the Marquis realised that the sarcophagus behind which they were hiding had been one of those brutally plundered in the past.

The top had been dragged off and smashed and the sides had been smashed too, so that in the light it would not give even the same protection that some of the others might have done.

It was just a question of time before they were seen, and the Marquis decided that it would be best for him to kill one of the men and keep his second bullet for a last stand if they should try to rush him.

Then he was aware of a strange, unexpected sound.

For a moment he thought he could not really have heard anything and that it was part of his imagination.

Then he was aware that the robbers were suddenly still and were standing listening to what he himself heard.

It was a very low, deep note, almost like the buzz of a bee. Then it became louder and it seemed so resonant and so insistent that it began to be taken up by the walls and the ceiling themselves.

It grew in intensity. It grew and grew until in absolute astonishment the Marquis, who had his arm round her, realised it came from Shikara!

It seemed to vibrate from the very depths of her body and all the time it was becoming intensified.

Now the sound seemed to be thrown back at them from the darkness and almost to hurt the ears of those who listened.

It was strange, compelling, and at the same time frightening.

It seemed as if the robbers were completely spellbound, as indeed was the Marquis.

Then suddenly with a cry of: "The gods! The gods!" Ali first began to run down the passage-way and the others followed him.

Still the haunting, vibrating sound came from Shikara until finally the candles which had gone with the plunderers or had become extinguished in the sand took away the last vestige of light.

Then there was only the darkness and the sound she had made quivering in the silence.

For a moment both Shikara and the Marquis were very still, until instinctively she turned towards him and his mouth came down on hers.

She knew that this was what she had been longing and aching for and once again she felt that her whole being merged into his.

She was still trembling, but it was no longer from fear.

Everything else vanished and it was impossible to

think of anything but the closeness of the Marquis's body, his lips, and him.

It was a kiss all the more intense, all the more poignant, because of the fear through which they had passed, and when finally he raised his head, she whispered, because she could no longer help saying the words:

"I love . . . you! I love . . . you!"

He pulled her against him. Then he said in a voice that was hoarse and a little unsteady:

"Let us try to get out of here, my darling, while we still can do so."

She felt a surge of happiness because of what he had called her.

But already he was moving from behind the sarcophagus into the passage-way, and blindly, holding on to him with one hand, she followed.

He bent down, struck a match, and lit the candle-lantern.

"We must be careful," he said, "very careful in case those plunderers are lurking outside."

"They . . . would have . . . killed . . . us!" Shikara said in a low voice.

"I was sure of that."

"They killed . . . Papa! The man called Ali . . . boasted of it."

"We must go very carefully," the Marquis said as he straightened himself, holding the lantern in his left hand. "All that matters now is that I should get you to safety."

He put his arm round her as he spoke and they moved slowly down the passage-way, the Marquis staring ahead. But Shikara's heart was beating tumultuously with joy.

He had kissed her! He had called her "darling"! She was close beside him and if they had to die at this moment she felt it would be of little importance.

"I love you! I love you!" she wanted to cry aloud.

But she knew he was anxious.

When they reached the shaft leading upwards he

went ahead and she saw that he had his pistol in one hand and the other hand was holding the lantern.

She followed behind him, and when there was enough light from the stars and the moon to show the way, the Marquis blew out his candle.

Shikara moved beside him into the entrance as he stood looking out through the broken pillars onto the desert outside.

There were the great boulders and rocks, and in the light from the moon they had a strange beauty which they did not show in the day-time.

Silhouetted against the sky was the Step Pyramid, but as far as they could see there was nothing moving, no human being in sight.

The Marquis slipped his pistol into his pocket, and taking Shikara by the arm hurried her as quickly as he could over the sand towards the palm trees where they had left their carriage.

The rough stones hurt her feet and sand trickled into her slippers, but she was not aware of any discomfort, only of a wild, ecstatic happiness.

It rose within her like a new-born phoenix after the depression and uncertainty she had felt when they drove here from Cairo.

They reached the carriage.

Their coachman, who was asleep at the foot of one of the palm trees, jumped up at their appearance, took from his horses the nosebags which had kept them quiet, and climbed onto the box.

The Marquis helped Shikara into the carriage, put the lantern down on the seat opposite them, and as the horses started off pulled her into his arms.

He felt her quiver against him and looked down at her eyes. He could see the expression of happiness on her face.

"You are safe, my precious one!" he exclaimed. "Tell me how you saved us. How could you make that incredible, unearthly sound?"

Shikara gave a little laugh of sheer happiness.

"Do you not know what it was?" she enquired.

"I have no idea," the Marquis answered, "and I cannot imagine how anyone as small as yourself could sound like a full orchestra from the depths of the earth, or perhaps from the heights of Heaven."

"It is the prayer of the Buddhist Monks," Shikara answered. "They sing, or rather intone, *Aum Mani Padme Aum.*

"But of course!" the Marquis exclaimed. "I know that it means 'Hail to the Jewel in the Lotus.'"

"And because every Monk intones it over and over again," Shikara explained, "it makes their voices deep and clear, and they never have any throat trouble, however old they live to be."

"How did you learn to do it yourself?" the Marquis asked.

"Papa taught me when I was very small," Shikara replied. "It amused me because it seemed to tickle the roof of my mouth and rise into my nose. He made me repeat it again and again until I could do it perfectly!"

Her voice deepened as she went on:

"I had almost forgotten it until suddenly when I heard those men saying they were going to ... search for ... us and if they ... found us we would be ... killed ... I knew what I must ... do."

The Marquis drew her close against him and kissed her forehead.

"You saved us both, my clever darling!"

She looked up at him and he said very gently:

"I love you! I have loved you for what seems to me a very long time. When I kissed you last night I was so afraid that you meant it when you said you hated men and in consequence would hate me."

"I love you!" Shikara answered. "But I knew you ... hated women, and I thought, although your kiss was the most ... wonderful thing that ever ... happened to ... me, it would mean ... nothing to you."

"It meant more to me than I can ever tell you," the Marquis said. "More than any kiss has ever meant. I knew then how much I loved you and that I had never been in love before."

He gave a laugh.

"I have fought against what I felt for you for a long time, Shikara, in fact all the time we were sailing through the Mediterranean."

"I wish I had known," Shikara murmured. "I knew that I ... loved you when we were in ... Lisbon."

The Marquis put his fingers under her chin and turned her face up to his.

"Were you jealous, my precious?"

"Terribly ... horribly ... jealous!" Shikara confessed. "It was something I had never felt before and it was very ... painful."

"There was no reason for jealousy," the Marquis assured her, "just as there will be no reason for you to be jealous of any woman in the future, because you, my most adorable little man-hater, are quite different from any woman I have ever known."

"Perhaps I shall just ... become like all the ... others now that ... I love you," Shikara whispered.

"You could never be like anyone else," the Marquis replied, "for the simple reason that I love you. I love you more than I can ever tell you! It will take me a lifetime to tell you how much!"

"Please tell me," Shikara begged.

Her lips were very close to his and he looked down at her for a moment before he deliberately kissed first her forehead, then her eyes, her cheeks, her small chin.

Finally, when she was longing for his lips so that she was trembling against him, his mouth found hers.

He kissed her wildly, passionately, fiercely, and she knew it was not only because he was excited but because it was a relief from the agonies he must have gone through when he knew that their lives were in danger.

"I love you! I love you!" she said over and over again.

She felt as if in some way they had both come back to life from a grave—the grave of the desert in which so many millions of people had died and were buried and which held so many secrets that would never be discovered.

But it was impossible for Shikara to think of anything except the feelings that the Marquis evoked in her and the happiness that seemed like a brilliant light with which they were both encompassed.

"I love ... you! I love ... you!" she cried.

The Marquis ceased kissing her only when they entered the streets of Cairo and there were houses and people on either side of them.

Shikara, however, held tightly on to his hand.

When they reached the yacht he stepped out first to lift her from the carriage and held her for a moment close against him.

Then they went aboard and into the Saloon.

The stewards hurried forward to attend to them and as Hignet appeared the Marquis handed him the pistol from his pocket.

"You had no trouble, M'Lord?"

"We are safe, thanks to Miss Bartlett," the Marquis answered. "But we have been through a very unpleasant experience, Hignet, and we both require a drink."

"The champagne's on ice, M'Lord."

"Then open it!" the Marquis commanded.

A steward poured out the champagne and only when they were alone in the Saloon did the Marquis raise his glass.

"To the bravest woman I have ever met!" he said gently.

Shikara looked at him and her eyes were shining like stars.

"I am not really brave," she answered. "You know how frightened I am of the sea, and I was very ... frightened indeed when I heard those men say they had killed Papa and would kill ... anyone else who ... interfered with them!"

"And yet you saved us!" the Marquis smiled.

"I think perhaps these things are ... ordained," Shikara said, her voice very low. "Perhaps all those

years ago, when I was a little girl, Papa was inspired
... or perhaps directed by something greater than
ourselves, to teach me to do what I did tonight so that
it would ... save both our lives."

"I am sure you are right," the Marquis agreed.

"Do you really believe that," she asked, "or are
you just saying it to please me?"

"I am telling you the truth," he answered. "I think
no-one could have come to Egypt and gone through
what we have without realising there are powers beyond ourselves, and there is a Force, whatever you
may call it, which can save or destroy us."

"It saved ... us."

The Marquis put down his glass and moved towards her. He pulled her once again into his arms as
he said:

"I love you! I have to keep telling you so because
it is a new experience for me to say these words and
to feel as I am feeling now."

"What are you feeling?" Shikara asked.

"Very, very much in love."

Shikara gave a little sigh of sheer happiness. Then
before she could tell the Marquis how much she loved
him he was kissing her again and it was impossible for
her to speak the words which were singing in her
heart.

Chapter Seven

Shikara stood at the window looking out onto the desert.

She had never thought that anything could look so beautiful as the three great Pyramids in the moonlight and a little way to the left of them the mighty Sphinx.

She had dreamt, she thought, that one day she would be able to look at the desert with the Marquis, but she had never imagined they would be staying here on the very edge of it and that it would be so magical.

There was just the Heaven above and the endless desert below.

They had been married in the Church next to the British Embassy and it was entirely due to the British Ambassador that they had been lent this enchanting Villa which stood on the very sand of the desert itself

It had been late when the Marquis had left Shikara the night before and she had gone to bed pulsating with the sensations his kisses aroused in her.

She was so unbelievably happy that she was half-afraid to sleep in case like a dream it vanished from her grasp and she awoke to find it was all untrue.

"You must rest, my darling," the Marquis had said tenderly, "you have been through a great deal today and I know you are tired."

144

"Not when I am with . . . you," Shikara answered.

"We have all our lives in front of us," he said. "I will spare you just for tonight, but after that we shall be together both by day and by night, so that I shall never lose you."

"You could . . . never do . . . that," she answered.

"I cannot be sure," he replied half-jokingly, half-seriously. "Perhaps you will leave me on the end of a rope, or disappear in the yacht of some unknown man, and I will never find you again."

She laughed, but she realised that beneath his words he was in fact intent on keeping her with him and it thrilled her to know that he cared enough and that she was essential to him.

As if he sensed her thought, he said quietly:

"Once you are my wife, I will insist that you will behave in a very much more circumspect manner than you have done until now. I am appalled at the risks you have run!"

"I would have been . . . frightened if . . . you had not been with . . . me."

She gave a little cry and said, holding on to him:

"Suppose . . . just suppose that if I had really escaped from you at the end of the Mews and that beggar had not stopped me . . . I might never have seen you again!"

"In which case," the Marquis said, "you would have gone on hating men and avoiding them until I found you again."

"You would not have looked for me!" Shikara replied accusingly.

"Perhaps not consciously," he answered. "But I think that ultimately we could never have escaped each other. It was fate, my precious one, that we should come together. Fate that we should fall in love!"

"It is not surprising that I should . . . love you,"

Shikara said a little humbly, "but that you should love me. . . ."

He turned her face up to his and he said:

"You are beautiful, you are brave, you are kind and understanding. What man could ask for more of one small person?"

"I want to be . . . all those things for you," Shikara said passionately.

He held her close, kissed her forehead, and said:

"Because I love you and because now I will take care of you for the rest of your life, I am sending you to bed."

She moved a little closer to him and whispered hardly above her breath:

"I do not . . . want to . . . leave you."

"And I do not want to leave you, my precious darling, but it is only for tonight."

"Do you . . . really mean we are to be . . . married tomorrow?"

"I made this afternoon all the arrangements for our wedding!"

Shikara stared at him in astonishment.

"This afternoon when you went ashore? I wondered where you were going. But how could you have known . . . how could you have been . . . sure . . . that I would . . . marry you?"

"Have you forgotten that I kissed you?" the Marquis asked. "I knew when your lips touched mine that we were meant for each other and that nothing and nobody could divide us."

He gave a sigh.

"At the same time, I was afraid! Even though I felt sure of your love, I was not certain that you would acknowledge it with your mind, and that you were not still hating me as you told me you hated all men."

"But you arranged to marry me?"

"When we had seen *Monsieur* Mariette I realised that your father was dead," the Marquis replied, "and because I knew how independent you were and, may

I say, regrettably unfeminine, I was afraid you might do something outrageous like run away from me."

Shikara gave an exclamation, remembering how desperately afraid she had been of having to leave him and how her whole being had yearned for him.

"I would ... never have left you ... willingly."

"How could I be sure of that?" the Marquis asked. "And I knew I had to look after you. Your absurd idea of earning your own living was quite impractical. You are too lovely, my darling, to be left alone in the world."

"So you arranged our marriage?"

"When I told the British Ambassador what had happened to your father, he agreed that we should be married immediately, and that he would see to all the documents and papers necessary."

The Marquis's arms tightened round her as he said:

"Leave everything to me. From now on you are my responsibility and I will not have you worrying about anything—except perhaps me!"

"I want to look after you ... I want to do things for you that no-one else can do," Shikara said.

"I shall keep you fully employed," the Marquis answered, "and your salary, my precious, will be paid in love and kisses."

She laughed at that. Then with a firmness that she accepted, he refused to discuss anything more but took her to the door of her cabin.

"Tomorrow night we will be together," he said, his voice suddenly very deep. "Sleep well, my lovely darling. I want you to look more beautiful on your wedding-day than you have ever looked before."

It would have been difficult not to feel both happy and beautiful, Shikara thought.

The Marquis's consideration for her in every detail made her realise how very different everything was going to be when she was his wife.

She was thankful that she had a very pretty white gown which she had bought in Lisbon and had not worn previously. It was in fact a dinner-gown, but not quite so elaborate or ostentatious as if it had been a Ball-gown.

The deep bertha was trimmed with little white flowers appliquéd onto lace and the same flowers decorated the flounces of the full skirts.

It made Shikara look very young and very innocent.

She was nearly dressed and was arranging her hair in the mirror when Hignet brought to her cabin a box which contained a very delicate lace veil, and with it a wreath fashioned from orange-blossoms and other white flowers.

It was, Shikara thought, exactly what she needed to make herself look like a real bride.

When a little shyly she had gone from her cabin to find the Marquis, he was waiting for her in the Saloon with a bouquet of the same flowers that were woven into her wreath, combined with lilies and white orchids.

She raised her face to thank him and he looked at her for some seconds before he said:

"You are not only beautiful, you are everything I ever longed for and thought never to find in my wife."

"I want to please you ... I want to do ... everything you ... want of me," Shikara said, "but ... suppose when you know me better you are ... disappointed?"

The Marquis smiled.

"I am prepared to bet a very considerable sum of money that we shall neither of us be disappointed with each other, but that our love will grow and intensify as the years go by."

He put his arms round her and added:

"You are very unpredictable, my adventurous one, and I shall always be afraid that you will find life with me so dull that you will be looking for adventures elsewhere."

Thinking of the fear she had felt last night, Shikara gave a little shudder.

"You know at heart I am a ... coward," she replied. "I do not want to be afraid ... but to feel ... safe with you ... as I feel now."

"I will look after you and love you for the rest of our lives," the Marquis said, "and I have a feeling that even when we die we will not be apart."

She had never known him to speak so seriously.

Yet when they were being married in the little English Church and they made their vows, Shikara knew that he was as deeply moved as she was.

Just as the Marriage Service was sacred to her, so it was to him.

She held very tightly on to his hand as they walked down the aisle together and when they were in the carriage driving away from the Church she laid her cheek against his arm and said very softly:

"I love you! I did not know it was possible to love you more than I did already, but I do!"

"I will tell you how much I love you in return," the Marquis replied in his deep voice, "but now, my darling, we have to go to the British Embassy for luncheon. I could not refuse the Ambassador when he invited us."

His Excellency had been a witness to their wedding and had followed them in another carriage.

Although Shikara longed to be alone with the Marquis, she realised that the fact that they must be entertained was one of the penalties of his important position.

The British Embassy was very attractive with a large flowered-filled garden, and although there was only a small party to celebrate their wedding it seemed to Shikara that it was a very gay one.

She and the Marquis were toasted by the Ambassador and everyone else present, and it was only when they were driving away that the Marquis told her that they were going not to the yacht, as she had expected, but to a Villa.

"We will spend three or four days there, or longer,

if you wish," he said. "But I want, my love, to have you completely alone."

When she saw the Villa, which, Shikara learnt, had been loaned to the British Ambassador by a Frenchmen who had returned to Paris, she realised that if she had had the choice she could not have wished for anything more perfect for her honeymoon.

The Villa had been built on the very edge of the desert and was a mixture of East and West, with the luxury of the latter and the exotic beauty of the former.

She exclaimed with delight over the exquisite rugs which decorated both the floors and the walls, and the statues and ornaments, many of which she was aware had come from the Tombs of the Kings.

Her bed-room was white and cool, and the wide deep bed, the soft rugs, and the ancient mirrors on the walls gave it an enchantment which told her it was the perfect setting for their love.

It was also fragrant with flowers sent there by the Marquis—lilies, orchids, and gardenias, which added a special magic to the dry wind blowing from the desert.

In the centre of the house was a cool courtyard where a fountain trickled over exotic plants, and the clematis and bougainvillaea grew over the walls in vivid profusion.

There were orange as well as pine trees in the garden, and small, secret places where they could sit alone, surrounded only by the scented shrubs, while just over the wall there stretched the dry sands.

As Shikara looked at the desert now, a great desolate sea of loneliness in the moonlight, she thought she could understand how the sands stretching away to the utmost horizon could create fear and even despair in some people's minds.

Then she realised that the Egyptians, who had always been preoccupied with the idea of death, as it had been said that the life of an Egyptian was always a journey towards it, had left in the Sphinx a symbol of hope.

It was a promise of life which many people might not understand.

She could see the outline of its strange shape and its damaged head.

It had been spoken of always as an enigma, but she felt, although she might be mistaken, that she knew what the Egyptians had intended when they built it.

To them their gods were personified by animals, and therefore they had made the Sphinx half-human and half-animal, meaning for those who understood that every person created was half-human, half-divine.

And what, Shikara asked herself, was the key to man's Divinity but love?

It was love which lifted him from the common-place towards a Heaven where he could realise the greatness of himself and the importance of life

And as the idea came to her she knew that she would never again feel alone or insignificant.

She had her allotted place in the universe, and what could have shown it more clearly than the pattern of events which had brought her to where she was now—the Marquis's wife?

Even as she thought of him, she heard the door behind her open and he came into the bed-room.

He saw her standing at the open window and crossed to her side.

For a moment as he reached her he saw in the moonlight her eyes and her whole face transfigured with an ecstatic happiness because he was there.

"What are you thinking about, my precious?" he asked.

Instinctively she moved closer to him and he could feel the soft warmth of her body through the diaphanous négligée which she wore.

"I was thinking of . you and of our ... love "

"Could either of us think of anything else today?"

"I was also thinking that I will never again feel insignificant or alone," Shikara said. "I know now what I have been seeking, although I did not realise it. Why I was restless and unhappy, and why I hated people simply because they were unable to give me what I required."

"Tell me what that was," the Marquis asked, although he knew the answer.

"It was love," she answered, "the love I have for ... you and which I think ... you have for ... me."

He laughed gently, then as his lips sought hers he said:

"If you doubt my love I shall have to prove it, and that is something I am only too eager to do!"

He kissed her, and she felt again the ecstasy he had aroused in her, the flame running through her body and the forked lightning she had known the first time he had touched her lips.

Now, because she was sure of his love, it was even more wonderful, more intense.

When the Marquis raised his head, she said a little incoherently:

"P-perhaps this has all ... happened before ... perhaps we have ... met and loved each other ... and that was why we felt ... incomplete until we ... were together again."

"That is what I feel and what I believe," the Marquis answered. "And that is why, my precious one, we can never lose each other. There will be no death where we are concerned, only a new beginning."

Shikara looked out at the beauty of the moonlight on the desert and said:

"There is so much you have to ... teach me ... so much for me to learn ... but I love you, and everything is easy, because for us the whole world is filled with ... love!"

The Marquis put up his hand to sweep her hair back from her forehead and as it fell over her shoulders he thought she looked like a Priestess who had come to him from a Temple.

Then the warmth of her body, the vibrations he could feel reaching out towards him, and the softness of her lips thrust from his mind every thought but his love for her and the fire that was rising within them both.

"I love you!" he said. "You are mine, my darling. Mine from now until eternity, and I will never let you go!"

He was kissing her again with a passion that was demanding and masterful, his lips fierce and possessive, and yet she was unafraid.

She knew that something glorious leapt within her to respond to his desire, but she knew too that spiritually they were one person.

She felt his lips on her neck and then he pulled her négligée and nightgown from her shoulders to kiss her breasts.

Her breath came quickly through her parted lips and her eye-lids felt heavy. She did not understand but only knew she ached and yearned for him to hold her closer still.

"I ... love ... you ... I ... love ... you."

It was hard to say the words and her voice was low and broken.

She put her arm round the Marquis's neck and his kisses made her feel as if the fire in him joined with the fire in herself and it was no longer possible to think but only to feel its burning insistence.

This was love in all its majesty and glory, a love fierce and tempestuous, a love as overwhelming as the desert itself, and yet a love which cast out fear.

"I love you! I adore you! God knows I want you!"

It seemed to Shikara that although she did not reply, the same words were echoed within her so that her heart spoke for her.

Then, with his lips holding her completely captive, the Marquis drew her away from the window and the moonlight into the soft, scented darkness.